A FAREWELL to the WAR WITHIN

A battle with reality

RUTENDO ALYSSA-JOY MUSHONGA

A Farewell to the War Within
Copyright © 2021 by Rutendo Alyssa-Joy Mushonga

All rights reserved. No part of this publication may be reproduced, distributed, or transmitted in any form or by any means, including photocopying, recording, or other electronic or mechanical methods, without the prior written permission of the author, except in the case of brief quotations embodied in critical reviews and certain other non-commercial uses permitted by copyright law.

Tellwell Talent
www.tellwell.ca

ISBN
978-0-2288-5045-8 (Hardcover)
978-0-2288-5044-1 (Paperback)
978-0-2288-5046-5 (eBook)

CONTENTS

The Beginning… 1

Welcome to Canada 7

The Descent: Going Downhill 16

Further Downhill 21

Pre-COVID-19 27

COVID-19 50

The Lockdown Experience 61

The Beginning of a New Start.. 71

THE BEGINNING...

Teenagers. We are the in-between people, and life throws a lot of hurdles at us. Being a teenager means you're not a kid anymore but it doesn't mean you're an adult, either. Sometimes I feel bad for the tweens about to embark on this emotional roller coaster. Tweens are kids between 9 and 12 years old; these kids want to be cool like the older teens. A lot of tweens hop the fence and get on the roller coaster before they even turn 13; they think everything teens go through is so cool, but little do they know it's a trap. Of course, there may be some people who love riding the roller coaster or who don't have it as bad as the majority of teens I know—I don't want to imply that it sucks for everyone. All I know is that I was barely a teenager when the ride started for me . . . and as much as I would've done anything to get off, the switch was hit and I was beholden to the law of inertia.

When I was a kid, I endured a lot of bullying, starting in the second grade. Other kids used to hate me and call me names, but back then it didn't actually bother me that much. Sure, it hurt, but after I told my grandparents whom I lived with in Zimbabwe at that time, they went to talk to the principal, which made the bullying stop. In Grade 3, the bullying started up again and I got crafty. I would steal money from my grandma's purse so that I could buy snacks from the tuck shop and give them to the kids who were bullying me. Giving the bullies snacks helped the bullying stop. One day I stole one hundred dollars and that's when I got caught and I was in big trouble. The bullying restarted, and I told my grandparents and they went to the school again.

I eventually moved to South Africa with my parents, but it didn't change anything. Every year I would be bullied—and not only was I getting bullied but my grades kept getting worse and worse. I made some friends but they didn't do anything when I was bullied. I learned the language most of the kids at my school spoke, isiZulu, but that was a bad idea because then I could understand when people were trash-talking me.

During my time in South Africa, I started getting crushes on other girls, but I didn't dare tell anyone because I knew I would just be bullied even more. I started lying to get out of trouble and forging letters to excuse myself from doing homework. There was a time I got bullied and one of the bullies insulted my father, saying something about him dying. My parents didn't do anything so I took matters into my own hands and wrote a letter from "my mom" addressing what one of the bullies said to me. The letter was written out of anger and immaturity, so everyone could tell that a child wrote it and I got in big trouble for that.

In another similar situation, there was an old lady who lived in our apartment block who used to pick on us kids—she acted like she owned the building. Everyone hated her, especially me, so I wrote a letter telling her exactly what everyone hated about her and I put it in her mailbox. All the bullying had turned me into a pretty mean kid and I definitely abused my ability to write.

As a kid I was scared of all of my dad's male friends. It wasn't always like that, but at some point I started feeling paranoid that maybe I would get molested or something. My dad's friends looked super scary, but they would sometimes bring puzzles for me, so I warmed up to them. I was still paranoid, though, and to this day, I don't know how those thoughts got into my mind at such a young age.

My childhood wasn't all bad. There are a lot of things that I miss about those days, like going to the gas station with my dad to buy Barbie CDs and watching cartoons with him and doing puzzles. During my time in South Africa, my relationship with my parents was okay but slowly falling apart. Because I had previously lied a lot, they didn't believe me when I said I didn't do something and I would get in trouble for things I didn't do. But at least I had my cousin, my mother's oldest sister's son—I will call him TJ.

TJ was my best friend. Yes, I had my brother, but my brother was violent and took everything away from me—my toys, my gadgets and such. With TJ, it was different; we had fun together. We loved watching and playing Power Rangers and we'd have sleepovers and watch episodes of *All Hail King Julien* or *Zig & Sharko* until midnight; we'd ride bikes together and draw and colour. When TJ started going to my school, I was so happy to have him around. He looked up to me because my grades kept getting better. He didn't know the things I went through before he moved to South Africa; TJ saw me as a good person who was always up for anything, whether it was building a fort or going rollerblading. I always spent New Year's Eve with TJ while our parents went out to bars or big parties. They'd leave the two of us alone, but would buy a bunch of snacks and food for us and I'd come up with a fun way for us to celebrate together.

With TJ, I worked on becoming the role model he saw me as. My mom and I had an okay relationship; it wasn't really a relationship because she was always going away for work and when she came back, the first couple of days would be fine but then she would inevitably start yelling at me, and her leaving again would be kind of a relief. I missed her when she was gone, of course, but it was the type of missing where you just want to see the person once and don't mind not seeing them again for a while. For a time, I stayed with my aunt Zee and dad and a maid. My aunt Zee and I had a great relationship; she was like my best friend and so was my dad. The maid, on the other hand, was annoying. All the maids we'd had before, I'd been able to get rid of, but not the one we had in 2017. I hated having maids because they would yell and tell me what to do, which, in my opinion, defeated the point of having a maid.

At school, TJ started getting bullied. I didn't want him to end up like me, but because we were almost seniors at the school at that time, we had enough power to silence the bullies.

The year 2017 was a great year. Some of my favourite times were when TJ and I were dropped off at his house and we'd come home to good food made by his mother, my other aunt, Tino. I loved Aunt Tino, too; she used to buy candy for us and we would watch Bollywood dramas together even though my dad complained that I was getting obsessed with them. TJ's mum was like a substitute mother to me. She was always so proud of me and I always wanted to make her proud. This was the year I also had my first big birthday party; it was after extra lessons on Saturdays and it was so much fun.

The only bad thing about 2017 was that people teased me about something that had happened the year before. In 2016, I had a crush on the new boy at school. I had told people I thought I could trust about it, but they ended up stabbing me in the back. On Valentine's Day, I gave this boy a note saying that I liked him. The teacher had stepped out of the classroom, and as soon as I handed the note to my crush, he ran outside. I chased him to get the note back because I was scared he was going to tell the principal. In retrospect, it wasn't love; I was just bored. I wasn't even upset that the boy didn't like me, I was just embarrassed that I'd chased after him. Everyone eventually stopped teasing me about it, but they definitely remembered it.

Thankfully, I mostly got over the embarrassment. I started a dance club and we even performed in front of the school. I also started taking piano lessons alongside one of my best friends. The hardest thing that happened that year was that my mother tried to kill herself. I didn't know what had happened at the time, but I saw the ambulance and my mom was crying. It was very scary. Someone went to my mom's room to talk to her while my cousin and I were told to go to bed. I was curious, so I set my iPad on voice record and left it in my mom's room where she was talking to the stranger. Unfortunately, when I took back my iPad to listen to what was said, I couldn't hear anything. My dad told me that my mom was just sick. She was eventually discharged from the hospital and, for a while, it felt like things were getting better, like my life was getting better, and I decided to get off the roller coaster because of how reckless it was. But when 2018 rolled around, I was tempted to hop back on . . . and I did.

At the beginning of 2018, I became a senior at my school, but although I was a senior, I was not a leader. Our school picked prefects and I wasn't one, I was a helper of the prefects. I wasn't upset about it, though, because I wasn't good with responsibility and I was still a helper, so I didn't really care. I was just happy that my grades were through the roof. We had started learning Grade 7 economic management sciences and I was in the top 10 in my class, so my aunts were very proud of me, which made me happy. It was also around this time that my best friend and I got into a huge fight. My best friend at the time was Nompumelelo—Nonie, for short. Nonie heard a rumour that I was saying mean things about her, but I wasn't. So she attacked me on WhatsApp and I attacked her back. I had recently gotten onto social media—it was basically just another means for me to wield my most effective weapon, which was the written word. We sent mean things back and forth. We both got in trouble at school because of this WhatsApp conflict, but we ended up making up with each other.

Another day, we had to stay after school because we had to finish our schoolwork that didn't get done that day; we had a lot of work to do. If it wasn't complete, we would get hit. My friends and I would often sneak into class early and copy each other's work just so we wouldn't get hit. That day was different. We were told if we were not done, we would get hit and get detention. Some people even missed their ride home because of that. Everyone was acting up that day: it was like a pub and people were jumping on desks and writing on the chalkboard. I was doing my work silently and fast so I wouldn't miss my ride home. When we got caught, the vice-principal said she would have to tell the principal and teachers about it. The next day all the prefects lost their positions and everyone blamed me, even though I had done nothing.

After school, all the other kids surrounded me and started yelling and throwing stones at me. I was crying on the ground and my uniform was dirty. When I got home, I was crying and I said I didn't want to go to school anymore and my dad said I could stay home for a few days. My aunt Zee reported the bullying to the principal and everyone got in trouble again. This was around the time when I got the news that we were migrating to Canada. When I went to school to pick up my things, I didn't expect that I would get an apology. All the students were forced to write a letter to apologize for what they did. It was forced, but I was a forgiving, naïve person back then and I immediately forgave them—besides, I knew I never had to see them again since we were moving to Canada.

WELCOME TO CANADA

On my last day of school in South Africa, I gave all my stuffed animals to my best friends and people signed my shirt. I was so excited about the plane ride to Canada—not because it was my first time on a plane, but because I just loved flying. I grew up going on planes to visit my parents or grandparents between Zimbabwe and South Africa and I enjoyed these trips. When we first arrived in Canada, I stayed with some of my mom's cousins whom I already knew from when they used to live in Zimbabwe and also when they visited Africa. There were three families of my mum's immediate cousins. The family we stayed with had a daughter, Tanya, who was three years younger than me, and she had a brother who was four years younger. At first, Tanya and I were good roommates but then we started fighting over small things like Barbies and jewellery. Sometimes it even got physical. I stopped playing with Barbies that year when I was 11 years old.

I noticed that one of my cousins, Natasha, who was a year older than me, was way more mature and cooler than I was and I wanted to be like her. Natasha and I were in the same grade, mostly because grades are different in South Africa than in Canada. I was so obsessed with Natasha: I wanted to dress like her, be smart like her, be funny like her and play basketball like her, but I eventually stopped looking up to her.

I wrote a story about what happened for a school project and I got an A for it. Here is the story:

Hello there. My name is Gaby. I am from South Dakota. I am 13 years old and I moved to Nebraska last year in 2017. I was enrolled in a school called Margaret Mills Middle School. Everything was great but I was a bit bored, so I decided to join rugby since it was my favourite sport. While I was enjoying rugby, I met three amazing girls, Natasha, Anna and Emma, who became my friends. We talked, then we officially decided to make the "She-Wolf Pack." It was a friend group on Instagram that was so relevant. I was so happy . . . until a girl named Olivia came.

I did not know or care about Olivia, but one day I saw her hanging out with Natasha and I was confused, so I called Natasha to come and sit with me because I was a bit jealous and I did not like when she sat with other people at school. She asked Olivia to come and sit with us but I had not agreed to that. I ended up being jealous of Olivia because she spent more time chatting with Natasha than me.

When I got home from school I called Natasha to ask about Olivia. When I called her, Olivia picked up. I asked her what she was doing at Natasha's house and she said, "I am here to hang out with my cousin Natasha."

I was so shocked that I brutally slammed down the phone and hung up.

The next day I was at school. I had to know if what Olivia said was true and it was. When I got confirmation from Natasha, I was worried about how rude I was to Olivia, so when I got home, I got her number from Instagram and talked to her.

Olivia said, "Hi, who is this?"

I answered, "It is Gaby, Natasha's best friend."

She remarked, "Oh the person who rudely hung up on me."

I said, "I am so sorry, my phone died."

Olivia replied, "It is okay, and anyways, if I am mad it will only last for two seconds. You know, I wish I was a cat because I would like to have nine lives so if I kick the bucket, I will come back to life. That would be so cool."

I said, "You know what? I would like that too."

Olivia said, "Got to go. Natasha is here to help me study for the quiz!"

Oliva was actually funny but not my type and when I mean not my type, I mean she was not what I look for in a friend.

The next week, we went to school and Natasha came and sat with us. She kept mentioning how Olivia was amazing and how she was an awesome dancer and I asked, "Do you think she is a better dancer than me?" and she answered, "Uh, am . . ." (bell rings). Natasha whispered, "Thank God I was saved by the bell."

After school I bumped into Olivia. She looked really scared and messed up. She immediately ran into the bathroom to hide. It was as if she was Flash's daughter, starring in Fast and Furious/Need for Speed. It was as if she saw a ghost. At home I FaceTimed her and asked her, "Why are you so afraid of me? I am not Medusa, you know," and she replied, "I am sorry. It is just when I see you I feel sick, not in a rude way."

I stated, "You don't talk to me and all Natasha talks about is how awesome you are. I would like to know you but you keep pushing me away."

Olivia said, " I will prove to you that I am not afraid of you. What do you want me to do?"

"You should hang out with me and my friends the whole day at school," I said.

Olivia replied, "Okay."

We had been speaking for half an hour and then she texted me a question she screenshotted from one of my best friends from South Dakota. I asked my friend why she added her and she said it was because she liked her Instagram account. I was angry that she had brainwashed my best friend, too, so in my anger I told Olivia that she was ugly and she did not have any friends. I also said her whole family was full of wimps. She defended herself but I cancelled her and said that she was not allowed to go near me or my *friends. I was upset that my day was horrible. My friend liked my nemesis and my crush liked my other friend. I shut off both Natasha's cousin and my other friend.*

Hi. I'm Olivia, and I will be telling part of my story. I will give you some of the reasons why Gaby is a bully, but I will tell you a bit about myself first. I am Olivia Emerald James. I am from Minnesota. I moved here this year. I moved here because my parents got jobs. I'm 12 years old and I love school. At first I was upset to leave Minnesota because my family and friends were there, but when I got here I was happy to find a new family and friends. Everything was fine until Gaby Smith came into my life.

At school I was sitting with my cousin Natasha. We were talking about the next quiz that was coming up. Gaby called Natasha to come sit with her. I found it rude because she saw that I was sitting with her. Natasha replied, "I'm sitting with Olivia. Can she sit with us?" and Gaby whispered, "No!" I heard her say no, but it seems my cousin is deaf and did not hear her. My cousin still asked me to sit with them and I obviously said no because who would want to be somewhere you are not wanted? I like being wanted, and when I say wanted I don't mean "wanted" as in you committed a crime.

When I went to my cousin's house I told my cousin about how Olivia didn't want me to sit with them. She was shocked but we put that in the past. After a few hours, Gaby called on my cousin's iPad and I answered. She asked me what I was doing at Natasha's house because she was clearly jealous and I told her I'm her cousin and I could be there anytime, and guess what? She hung up on me. But I didn't care because I didn't want to get distracted since I was studying.

At school I was walking down the hall and I saw Gaby and hid. She kept on talking about how she was so popular. She really has a high self-esteem and that is the other reason why she is a bully. I honestly think that Gaby is full of herself.

Two weeks later, we were doing our Grade 7 midterms. I was so prepared that I found the test very easy and everything was good. I was confident about my marks, but I thought wrong. I was told that I got twenty-five per cent on my math and I knew that Gaby had done something, and I was right because she texted me, "Now how do you like being sabotaged the way you sabotaged my friendship?" but I was curious as to how she hacked into the computer since she was as dumb as a cat. I was so angry because I didn't sabotage her, I was just telling the truth. Let me tell you how this sabotage thing started.

On the 5th of April, my cousin went to a rugby competition in California and I went with her to watch. They lost two times and had one game left on the 6th of April. Gaby was also on the team but that didn't bother me; just because her presence makes me paranoid doesn't mean I can't enjoy life. Life goes on.

So, the team and their families were invited to Montana Joe's for dinner. It was a bit awkward. My other cousins and I wanted to sit with Natasha and she was sitting with her team, which made it a bit hard for us to communicate because, awkward, but we still managed to pull it off that night. Like they always say, "Sticks and stones may break my bones but people won't"—oh, those are the wrong words. Anyway, it was their final game and they FINALLY won! We were all happy. They celebrated and we went back to Nebraska. A few weeks later, it was my birthday, April 29th. I was so happy that the same day was the spring dance and Natasha and I went all out like the time in March when it was the seventh grade dance. It was awesome. The day was great . . . until I found out my birthday was on the same day as my cousin's best friend's birthday. Then I got angry because Natasha was supposed to attend my sleepover AND she was supposed to attend Gaby's birthday party. It was not great because she double-booked and my sleepover was the next day and hers, too, but I decided to wish Gaby a happy birthday to be kind and let this issue be the next day's issue because I really didn't want to ruin my day. So, I pulled my guts up and wished her a happy birthday but there was also another issue: I spilled coffee on her dress for the dance and she couldn't go home and come back in time because she lived far away from the school. She had to go like that to the dance. It kind of made me smile to see the person who hates me so pressed, but I also felt guilty.

Over all, my birthday went well. I embarrassed the most popular girl at school and got Natasha to go to both parties because it was the least I could do since I ruined Gaby's dress. But it was her face that was hilarious. I couldn't help breaking out and laughing. Then it was finally the day I'd been waiting for: my birthday sleepover. We had water fights and watched The Babadook *by Jennifer Kent*. It's a horror movie. We ate McDonald's and had a lot of fun. However, when I was checking my social media I saw a message from Gaby saying, "Olivia James, why do you hate me?"

I replied, "I don't hate you. I thought you hated me. You were being mean and throwing shade at me."

Gaby answered, "I only do that because when I approach you to try to talk to you, you run away like you witnessed bloody murder!"

I called her so I could actually hear her voice. She said, "You had a lot of chances to talk to me but you were being immature and ignorant!"

I replied, "I'm being ignorant and immature? You are the ignorant, obnoxious and immature person here. My cousin asked me to sit with you but you said no, which shows you didn't want me there. I don't wanna fight. I'm trying to enjoy the rest of my birthday weekend, so don't spoil this for me." I hung up and went to bed.

The next day I saw ten messages on my phone on a group her other friend who I talk to a lot (Anna) made. The messages were attacking me, which was scary. I asked for help but my family didn't care. They said I was fighting a lot with Gaby. I was tired; I cried a lot. She was judging me about how I look and how I'm a ginger and then my family attacked me, too. I didn't feel like they were my family. Gaby kept calling me and stalking me and trying to hurt my feelings. I'd had enough. I was so depressed because everyone was attacking me. I kept asking myself why I was put on this earth as a target. I had no one on my side except two of my little cousins but they really couldn't do anything but try to help. I felt hopeless. I decided to just tell them that she was making fun of how I looked and then they realized *that they were not acting like family. My cousin Natasha wanted to break bonds with her. I said no. I don't know why I kept saving Gaby but I did, and that is one thing I loved about the experience of being bullied by her. Natasha then confronted her, and Gaby acted like she never said any of it.*

I had another experience like this when my cousins travelled to Hawaii. I sent a message to the family group chat telling them to make sure Natasha didn't break off her friendship with Gaby, and they started attacking me, saying I convinced her to break off their friendship but I didn't. I was just trying to save their friendship and they kept accusing me. I didn't know who was bullying me worse at that point, Gaby or my family!

Gaby is a nice person. She is nice to everyone but me, and I understand why everyone hates me because I don't belong in their world.

Hello readers, I am Natasha. I will be telling you how my family worked together to make my cousin Olivia feel better about herself and forget the troubles she got into. I once had a bet with my best friend, Gaby. She won and she said I should bully my cousin Olivia and I did. It was so dumb of me to do that to my family but I mended my mistakes. Olivia is a great person. The family loves her a lot. I mean, yes, we caused a lot of trouble for her. It was not a really good welcoming to Nebraska but we managed to fix our mistakes. I told her, "Olivia, you are an amazing person. The family loves you for a million reasons. We made mistakes and you did, too, but we still love you. We didn't mean to make you feel like you were being attacked or make you feel upset. We wanted to help you 'cause we love you."

She replied, "I was mistreated. I was attacked. Everyone caused me pain. I will forgive but not forget, 'cause if anyone hurts me, I will always forgive but not forget. I am also sorry for making you worry because of the condition Gaby put me in, and I know I'm emotional and I exacerbate my problems, but I would never choose anyone over my family, not even my best friend. But you did, which hurt me, but let's not bring it up again."

I could tell she was in pain but I knew she would come around eventually.

The End

I wrote the story with different points of views. I have to admit that I do not know what any of the other people in the story were actually thinking or feeling, but I do know that for a while I felt dejected. Natasha did apologize but to this day I'm still hurt by what she did. What she did in simple terms is she said terrible things about me because of a dare made by a bully. Sometimes I feel like some of the things she said were true. I was obsessed with becoming like her and I guess she got annoyed and hated me for it. In the story, I also wrote how I think Gaby, the bully, felt; she felt jealous and like an outsider stepped onto her turf. And because my cousin apologized, I feel that she was sorry, too. I forgave everyone in the end like I always do, but that was the first crack in my heart.

I had my first Halloween and dance in 2018; things were great. I was getting used to life in my new country, but the way I dressed up was still childish. I also went to a summer camp for the first time. There was a strict owner who picked on everyone but her grandson, but we managed to have a good time that summer. Later on, we had to move to a smaller place because my mom got a job. We moved from Fort McMurray to Little Lacombe. I continued writing but I did not use it as a weapon anymore, I used it to get good grades.

In Lacombe it was all different. We lived in an apartment and I went to a smaller school. I made a friend, Anna, on the first day. Anna was nice and we always hung out. Later on, I found out she smoked and I stopped hanging out with her, then I made a few other friends. I joined basketball for the first time and I was pretty good. I got closer to two people on the basketball team and they became my best friends. A lot of people knew me and wanted to be friends, especially those in the younger grades. After a while, Anna wanted a second chance and I gave it to her, but I should have known that it was a bad idea.

My new friends and I went to hang out with Anna at the library and she ditched us to sit with her other friends. Anna took the snacks I bought and shared them with her friends who started throwing them at us. She then went to smoke with her friends. They were locked outside and you could only open the door from the inside and they expected us to open the door even after she'd ditched us. They were finally able to get in and then they started trash-talking all of us. Stupid me went over with a cup of Sprite and threw it at the person who was talking all the smack and they called me outside and I went. I recorded the whole conversation. They were just making threats like, "I'll knock your teeth in if I ever see you in the street." Afterwards, I went home and got on Snapchat.

I had earned enough respect to be added to the class group. School was like jail: in order to be accepted and respected, you had to do something big. In the Snapchat group, I explained everything that happened and uploaded the voice message for everyone to hear, but I didn't know that Anna was also in the group. She saw the messages and the evidence and still denied it and then everyone attacked her. I didn't because I knew how it felt. Plus, Anna had a hard life; her parents were divorced and she lived with her grandparents because she ran away a lot. The situation escalated after Anna's friends were added to the group and they made threats, and threats were thrown back and forth. One of my friends, Debra, told the principal about it and we all got in trouble. The police were involved because of the cyberbullying that was taking place. My parents were so disappointed in me, mostly because I didn't tell them about the issue in the first place and they had to hear it from the authorities. Everyone was not very friendly with Anna and she eventually stopped coming to school.

I should have noticed certain things when all of this drama happened. Anna wasn't really involved, it was her friends who started it. She was just a bystander in the situation and everyone took it out on her. I also didn't do anything about how Anna was treated. I just watched and walked away. And now she wasn't coming to school anymore. I was complicit.

THE DESCENT: GOING DOWNHILL

It was my first winter in Canada, when I noticed myself getting depressed and feeling worthless. I thought maybe it was just seasonal depression and it would pass, so I brushed it off. I started having feelings for my best friend, Debra, who was Mexican, but she didn't know. When we had our first sleepover with our other best friend, I wanted to tell Debra about my feelings but she was talking about a guy she had a crush on, so I didn't. Eventually, some days after the sleepover, I got the guts and told her, but I said that I would get over it. She was my first real crush.

I made another friend, Holly, and she was really cool, nice and artistic, but my depression got worse and I started cutting my wrists. I felt alone. I talked to Debra and she told me that she was going through a similar situation and advised me to see the school counsellor. I went to see the counsellor and said she had to tell my parents about my visits just to make sure she was not overstepping. My parents were flabbergasted by what they heard from the counsellor and they yelled at me. They didn't understand anything about what I was going through. My parents yelled at me so much that school became my haven. I would go to the bathroom and cry my lungs out. The big, wheelchair-accessible bathroom stall was a safe space for me. It was where I took out my emotions, where I could escape from everything.

 I remember the first time I went into the big bathroom stall in the girls' bathroom at school. I had gotten into a fight with Debra and I felt so scared and humiliated. I ran into the washroom and all the stalls were full, excluding the big one. I didn't know what was so extraordinary about it at first. I went in and sat with my back against the wall and my arms wrapped around my knees. I cried my eyes out and all of a sudden I was lost in my emotions. I remembered all the positives as well as the negatives; I felt like I was flying. I felt free.

 In 2019, I went skiing for the first time in my life and I hated part of it so much. I got so depressed. I talked to Debra's crush boy and he wasn't bad, but he said that Holly had led Debra to have suicidal thoughts. I got so angry and told him off, which made Debra mad. I made up with him for Debra's sake, and we started talking more. In the beginning, he was helpful with the whole depression situation but then one day he stopped being helpful.

 I was at the movies with Debra watching *Avengers: End Game* and I had a panic attack. I texted him and he calmed me down. I don't know why I texted him when my best friend was right next to me, but I did. When I got home, I called Holly and I told her what happened at the movies and she stayed on the phone with me. She had always done that when I was having a mental breakdown. She would tell me stories until I fell asleep, but this time she was on the phone with me until the police called me. Apparently someone had called them saying I was going to commit suicide. I had no intention whatsoever of killing myself, but I knew exactly who called the police on me. The cops told me that it was Debra's crush boy and I told them that it wasn't true, and then we fixed the misunderstanding. I was so mad and I told Holly about it. My old friends made a plan to sabotage my Debra and her relationship and told Holly, who told me. They wanted to wait until the next day but I was too angry to wait. I decided to take it into my own hands, and Debra was so angry at me after but we later made up.

We all joined badminton and I went to all the practices. During one practice I had another mental breakdown. I went in the big stall and took out my headache pills. I used to carry the headache pills because I would get bad headaches whenever I was on my period. I swallowed six of them as an attempt to end the pain but didn't continue because I suddenly remembered my little cousin TJ in South Africa. My cousin wouldn't want this for me and I would be a bad role model. I told Debra and she told the principal who told my mom who told the cops who took me to the hospital. I was transferred to a hospital in Red Deer and released on the third day. I learned a lot of things from this experience but not how to control myself.

When I got out of the hospital I was worse, but I was way better at faking that I was okay. I started seeing a professional therapist and I liked her. I then isolated myself and broke off my friendships without thinking. I apologized but no one forgave me. People started talking badly about me. There was another girl who hated me and said I was using my mental health as an excuse and that I was just a drama queen. Part of what she said was right. I noticed that everywhere I went, there was drama and I was part of it. I wrote a long letter to apologize to Debra and she showed everyone. My therapist told me that she was like the Queen Bee in our class—like in the film, *It's a Girl's World* by Lynn Glazier—and my therapist also told me that I should do my best to stay out of that social hierarchy.

After that, people still talked about me but I tried to move on. I continued hanging out with some people who had forgiven me. I invited them over to my house to "study" and we talked, made slime and just had a good time . . . so I thought. One of the girls got on a call with Debra and they were gossiping about me in *my* house, which made me livid, but I tried to brush it off and move on.

One day, I had been cutting after coming home from the hospital and my arms were bleeding. Holly noticed and gave me her hoodie. A few minutes after, I had to leave to see my therapist so I left her hoodie in her locker, which was open, but she lost it and blamed it on me and said I had to pay for it. Track and field came and I was all alone. I told Debra that if she had something to say about me, she had to say it to my face, then Holly came over and called me a bitch. I went to the bathroom to cry and I texted my mom to come and get me and she said she would be there in a bit. My next-door neighbour who was my age but in a younger grade walked into the bathroom and asked me what was up and I told her. She and her other friend distracted me and we threw Freezees at each other. I decided to walk home and I told my mom what happened and she told me Debra had texted her asking her to come and watch me do track and field. I said she was two-faced.

I decided to keep myself busy to get my mind off things. I began hanging out with some of the girls I met at track and I started mentoring a girl in the second grade. I also started to hang out with a guy who lived near my street whose name was Mark. Mark would always buy Mike & Ikes for me because he knew I loved them at the time. We met by the trash cans. I was taking the trash out in my onesie and he commented on how nice it was. I was super cranky that day and I said, "Yeah, very funny," and he replied, "Who peed in your cereal?" and I said, "I'm just angry at my fate," and he asked, "Why is that?" and I replied, "Because every time a guy talks to me, I'm either wearing or doing something weird." Mark asked for my phone number and I gave it to him because he was interesting to talk to and I wanted new friends. I was feeling lonely and needed someone who was real to talk with.

We talked a lot but one day Mark told me he liked me and wanted to be more than friends, but I told him I liked someone else. He stopped replying to my texts and answering my calls and I felt bad. Mark had abusive parents and used to be addicted to drugs but had gone to rehab for it. I started worrying that he would go back to doing drugs, so I went to visit him at his house. It was a bad idea. When I went over to his house to apologize, he yelled at me and shoved me into a glass table. After that, I limped for a while and I stopped talking to him.

    Mark started posting about me on my TikTok account. I had given him my password because I thought I could trust him. He posted that I was a slut. I deleted it and changed my password. It took me some time to get over what happened. I had to forgive him because he had it hard and I knew how it felt to be hit by your parents for no reason.

FURTHER DOWNHILL

There was a time when I started taking sleeping pills for my insomnia. When my mom found out, she told me not to do it again. The next day she saw another pill was missing, but I didn't take it and she hit me anyway. I decided to take my bike to school instead of riding in the same car as her; it was like an angry husband and wife situation where the husband sleeps on the couch. Actually, the sleeping pill incident happened before my suicide attempt in the school bathroom. My mom's heart was in the right place.

At the end of the school year, I got a certificate for mentoring and I decided I wanted to go to a new city and start over. Before the move, I went to summer camp at Gull Lake—it was fun. I went tubing for the first time. The unfortunate thing was that I was on my period. I improved my painting skills at Gull Lake and I met a sweet girl. After camp she asked me to be her girlfriend and I said yes; she was the first person I dated in my life. It only lasted three days because she started stalking me, wanting to know everything I was doing.

That summer I also went to visit Fort McMurray, where I used to live. Before that trip, I had come out to my parents out of anger about how I was bisexual and also an atheist. They were so mad. During the trip, my mom said a lot of homophobic and hurtful things like "It's just a phase" and "You're just confused." She also said, "You shouldn't get married because if you get divorced you will kill yourself." The drive was horrible, but once we were there I was fine.

A couple of times during the summer we went to Edmonton. In Edmonton, I went to my cousin's soccer game and my first buffet. When the school year started, I immediately made new friends at my new school. My best friends at my new school were Elaine, Kim and Sally. We became friends through our appreciation of anime and dirty jokes. I was closest to Kim at the beginning. Kim and I were known in the hallways for doing stupid things. We all had at least one elective together so we were almost always together; we ate each other's lunches, we bought food for each other and we were friends with the same people. Kim and I walked with our arms looped through each other's elbows everywhere we went—you wouldn't see one of us without the other. If we were assigned group work, it was a no-brainer. We always worked together.

I started getting involved with boys. Elaine helped me score my first boyfriend. To be honest, before I moved to Red Deer, I dreamed that I would have the perfect life there—meaning that I would have lots of friends and a sweet boyfriend, just like in the movies, but only one of those things came true. The first guy I ever dated said "I love you" on the first day we went out together so it didn't last. I made some other friends who were two years younger than me and we went shopping together and I spent money on them. When my mom found out, she was mad. I didn't spend money on them so they would like me, they liked me already. One of them happened to bed my boyfriend and we had the same best friend and it only made sense that we all hang out together.

We used to hang out at the mall before my trip to Zimbabwe. One time we were chased around by some high school seniors. The guys thought it was funny but we were scared to death. My friend winked at them and we got scared; once we lost them, we went and played on the escalator. We did a TikTok trend of touching people's hands who were going down while we were going up. We also pretended to fall to see other people's reactions.

The second guy I dated was two years younger than me and it lasted three months, but it was weird for other people. He was the cute guy in his class and lots of girls were trying to score his attention, and I got it with a finger click. I was a little unpopular with the other girls until I broke up with him. I didn't break up with him just because of other people, though; I broke up with him because he cheated. While I was in Zimbabwe, he texted my best friend who was his best friend that he wanted to have sex with her. When I got back, I broke up with him.

In Zimbabwe I had a great time. I found out so much tea on others that made me look better. It was bad, but I was glad that I wasn't the one wearing the troublemaker title this time. I found out that my cousins were into all sorts of mischief, and one of them posted semi-naked pictures of themselves on Facebook. I honestly wasn't surprised about the situation; I was only surprised that I heard about it from a seven-year-old.

When I came back to Canada, it was freezing. I was still very close with Kim and we did everything together. I then started dating someone a year younger than me, one of my guy best friends. He was a goofball and so funny; everyone knew about our relationship, even the teachers. The teachers always smiled when they saw us together. I still don't know why we broke it off. On Valentine's Day he bought my favourite chocolate for me, a card and a unicorn stuffed animal. He didn't know what I liked so he asked Kim—when I say I almost fainted, I mean it.

The day before Valentine's Day, I volunteered to hide paper hearts at the school; each heart had the name of a person at our middle school on it, and the students had to find them and present them to the office to get candy. I was in charge of the Grade 6 and 7 names and I knew everyone, so I was a bit cruel about it. My name was put on my boyfriend's locker and his on mine; when I found it, I just rolled my eyes. After a month we broke it off. I started talking to a guy from New Zealand and Kim started talking to a guy from the US who she found on TikTok. I didn't like the guy Kim talked to and she didn't like the guy I talked to. That is where things fell apart. Kim started dating her guy and I said I approved but I didn't like him, and I started dating my guy and she approved but she actually didn't like him either. I wrote a story about this when it happened.

Has your best friend ever hurt you before? Because mine has. I am Rebecca. My friends call me Becca. I am 13 years old and I have a best friend named Khloe. Khloe is 13 years old, too, and we go to the same school. We used to be best friends and we were always together. Khloe and I had planned our future. We were going to go to the same university in Poland and live together with a cute dog but it all changed.

During the break I had gotten a new Internet friend. I told her not to say anything to anyone because my friend (Austin) didn't like that much attention, but Khloe didn't listen to me and she told Ava but I let it go because Ava was also my friend.

Later on that day we had recess and I hung out with Ava and Khloe. Brandon, the guy who had a crush on Khloe, came over to us. I didn't really like Brandon, mostly because he was clingy, and every time I looked at Khloe, he always had his arms around her. It was too much because Khloe already had a boyfriend. I mean, I understand that Khloe hugs all of her friends but not as much as Brandon does. Sometimes Brandon body-checked us to make us go away from Khloe and it made me feel uncomfortable.

After recess that day I told Khloe that she should tell Brandon to stop being so clingy, but she said she couldn't. Khloe used to say she didn't like the attention but I started to think she did because if she didn't, she would have told him to back off. Later on that day, we went to gym and we were still talking about Brandon but then Khloe brought up Austin. She said a lot of mean stuff about him and how I met him online. Khloe also said, "Are you that depressed and lonely that you have to get a boyfriend who lives that far away?" I got upset because I trusted her with my depression and she used it against me. I hated her then and I still do. Now we don't talk at all. She was my best friend—losing a best friend is harder than losing a boyfriend. A best friend is half of you, maybe the better half of you. A best friend advises you with your best interests in mind. Your best friend should be there for you and support you, even though what you're going through might be stupid. And last but not least, your best friend has to love you. Right now I'm still recovering from it all and it gets harder and harder by the day because we were inseparable. Everything hurts right now. I have been through a lot of breakups but it never felt as painful as this.

It didn't end up like that. In real life, I did a horrible thing: I told people on her and they turned against her. I was in the same group as her for science and she plagiarized an assignment; she also left me hanging and I presented it all by myself. I eventually came to my senses and I forgave her and she forgave me. It wasn't the same, though. Kim ended up moving back to her home town in El Salvador and I started hanging out with Elaine and Sally more. I had started taking taekwondo and contemporary dance in addition to basketball, but in February I had to quit both because I wanted to be in the ski and snowboard club more, and basketball practices clashed with taekwondo. The reason I joined taekwondo was because back in Lacombe before I moved I was sexually harassed by an old man; he wanted me to go with him in his car. I wanted to protect myself. I joined snowboarding because of Elaine. We had so much fun.

During basketball season when we went to the away games, my teammates would send me to get numbers from guys or girls they liked. It all started when we went on a field trip to the Calgary Zoo. Someone wanted a guy's number and I took her phone and went up to the guy to ask him for her. I didn't know that it would become something I was known for: suddenly everyone wanted me to score guys for them. Some of the guys at the zoo were hitting on Elaine and me but refused to give me their numbers. The boys were being jerks and making comments about her weight. I got mad because the girl was my friend, so I started ranting and yelling at them.

On the snowboard trip I went off on the Australian instructor, screaming that he wanted to kill me. In my defence, I was on my period and I was angry. Elaine cooled me off by giving me cramp medicine and I apologized to the instructor. Elaine and I started hanging out more. We would talk to each other on the phone for at least an hour every day. We hung out at the community centre, we went to movies and she taught me how to skateboard.

Back at the beginning of the year, I had a massive crush that lasted for a long time. The guy I liked started trying to control me and I showed him that he had no right. I hated him for telling people to stay away from me after that. I started bullying him. I kicked him and posted mean things about him—like if there was a purge, I would kill him first. I eventually realized that I was not being a good person and I got him a bunch of snacks to apologize and I deleted the posts.

PRE-COVID-19

Sometimes you can be bullying someone without realizing it. Before schools were closed as a result of Covid-19, I got bullied because of my skin and my outfits. The boys in my class made comments about me. I started feeling sad about everything and cutting again. I told my boyfriend about it. I told him I felt like drowning myself and he got worried and told Elaine. Elaine was worried and she told the counsellor who told my parents, and when I got home they asked me questions. I told them about my boyfriend but they didn't know who he really was to me. My parents told me I either had to stop talking to him or delete all social media. Out of anger I deleted all social media. I went to bed crying; I cried the whole night. In the morning I went downstairs because I was called to eat and I didn't talk or greet anyone, because I was still angry that my phone had been taken away. I stood in front of my parents, listening to them tell me how disrespectful I was and how I was making everyone miserable. I was trying my best not to cry but everything that they said hurt. They said that if I didn't want to be there, I could leave, so I tried but they stopped me. They ended up pinning me down and calling the police. After I talked to the police they said I could go if I wanted, as long as I wasn't doing anything illegal, and after they left, I walked to Elaine's house.

Elle and her parents let me stay with them and we had so much fun together. We watched movies until it was late, we cleaned their house, and for the first time I thought that cleaning was fun! Kim came over and we made TikTok videos and got slushies and I helped her with her paper route. Elaine's family was so welcoming and they even offered that I stay with them for good. Things were good, but the little visits my mom kept making where she would threaten me and Elaine's family were so annoying that I decided I had to leave. I asked someone to call the cops to take me to a shelter, and they did. When I went to the shelter, we came to the decision that I should go home, which I did. I went home and I was allowed to talk to my boyfriend again. A few days later, I got into a fight with him about having kids. I told him that in the future I didn't want kids because it would be selfish of me. I felt like I would be a terrible mother and besides being a terrible mother, I felt like my child would be a danger to society, because he or she could be like me. After that conversation he broke up with me. I did not take it very well. I went through all the stages of grief: denial, anger, depression, acceptance and getting over it. The denial lasted five days. Later on, I found out that while I was dating him, he asked another girl for nudes—that's when the anger kicked in. When I confronted him about it, he denied it, but when I showed him proof, he started threatening suicide. I told him not to do anything stupid and we blocked each other. I then entered the depression stage. Technically, I didn't enter depression because I already had it. I just became ten times more depressed than before.

There was a time after the breakup when I stopped eating and sleeping and I was underweight. I had more breakdowns and I cut so much more. When my mom yelled at me for not opening the door in my room while I was having a breakdown, I was done. When I came out, she took the door off its hinges and I started spending all my time in the closet. My grandma was mad at me for being so stubborn and I felt like a disappointment. So, I tried to kill myself again. I drank a whole bottle of vodka and grabbed a razor and a knife, but I missed my chance. I left the door open and my dad stopped me. The ambulance was called and they took me to the hospital. I stayed in the emergency and the next day the doctor came. The doctor said I needed individual therapy, family therapy and antidepressants. I agreed to do everything that he said just to get out of the hospital. My mom was feeling guilty about everything, so I wrote her an explanation.

Explanation (Version I)

I just thought you deserved an explanation to why my life is so messed up. I don't know where to start. It's like a whole long list of things bother me; sometimes I don't even know how to explain how I feel. Let me start by telling you why I don't tell you things. I don't say or talk about how I feel most of the time because in Lacombe, after coming out of the hospital, I isolated myself because I was scared that I was burdening my friends. You said that if I told them how I felt they would pull away, but in this situation I pulled away because of the fear of losing them. Because of me pulling away, they turned against me and said that I was using depression as an excuse. So, I stopped talking about my feelings because in other people's eyes, it's just excuses. And since we moved here, I talked about my feelings to Elaine and she was there to listen and that's what friends do. I told Kim because Elaine started drifting, not because I told her my feelings, but because I stopped opening up to her. I had stopped telling her about how I feel because you had said I was burdening them, so I closed up. I put on a fake face. I talked to Kim and she knows about putting on a fake face, and because I became friends with my Icelandic friend, Kim flipped and used my depression against me and we stopped talking, and because of what she did, I told Elaine about the mean things Amanda and Kim said about Sally and Amanda.

After drifting from Elaine, she still helped me through the drama with Kim and Amanda. Mom, you were right: Amanda is toxic, but I can't help that I forgive and let people in easily. As for Kim and me, I forgave her but we are not as close as we used to be. Kim and I planned to go to the same high school and then move to Norway together and visit on holidays, and possibly our families could celebrate holidays together, but all that went down the drain. But Elle was there for me.

I also don't come to you because what if I didn't have parents to help me with my problems? When I'm older I won't be able to depend on you guys and that scares me. You guys used to fight my bullies for me, but I have to learn how to do it myself. Sometimes I think maybe I should just live in the streets and learn how to be a real person with real, hard work to do, not simple chores like dishes and cooking. I want to study culinary arts in university. I haven't told you that before because I know you guys have your hopes up that I will be a doctor or writer. Sometimes I get really discouraged and I question my worth. Sometimes when I cook, you say I don't cook well. Sometimes I don't eat the food I cook because I feel like it's not going to be good enough.

Last year in Lacombe before we moved, you sent me to take out the trash and this old man drove by in his car and commented about my body and that led me to wearing hoodies often and staying inside. As time went by, I kept trying to build up my self-esteem by requesting to wear tube tops and short skirts, and I was trying to make myself feel better about how I looked, but that was hard.

I felt like I needed to do this alone because what if you guys weren't here? I wish we had one of those mother-daughter relationships on Instagram but I don't think we could ever have that because of my mood swings. I'm an overthinker. It's hard for me to sleep because I overthink things. Sometimes I close my eyes to try to sleep but then I just start thinking about how to make my life less miserable and more organized and I write those things down but then I lose hope.

The boys at my school made me miserable but I hid how I felt because if I showed that I care I would feel weak and hopeless and like I can't feel like that because that would just add another reason to why living is pointless.

I question life and the point of it all. I get into deep thought about faith and why scientists don't believe in it because scientists are right about most of the things they discover. Sometimes I think that we are all being mind-controlled. Sometimes I worry, what if I'm psychotic and I need to be in an institution? I get paranoid in the dark because I feel like my depression is going to drag me to my death. That's why I keep all the lights on in my room. I don't like being outside at night because I'm scared that because of my body, I'm going to get myself raped.

The worst feeling is being surrounded by people who love you but still feeling alone and unloved. I distribute love and never get the same amount back but it doesn't bother me that much because I'm mostly focused on my body and other insecurities.

When I said I didn't mind you guys being at my basketball game it wasn't to guilt-trip you but it was because I get bad anxiety attacks before playing, but while playing I stop thinking, which is why I love basketball. I don't talk about my anxiety because no one would understand and people would just say, "Sleep on it," or "Tomorrow will be better," or "That's life." People say, "I'm here for you," but they are not and it's not comforting whatsoever and people only say it because it's what the doctors say helps. I say, why bother explaining how you feel when no one will ever understand?

I cut to get a little bit of control over what I felt because I felt out of control. I didn't do it to be sent to the hospital. I hated being there. It made me feel more alone than ever, and trapped. Alcohol helped me numb the feeling, emotionally and mentally, and I was kind of hoping that I'd get so wasted that I would get the guts to actually end my life. Weed helped me calm down. I wanted a dog so bad because I read that dogs help support you emotionally, and it would be like a friend who I could pour my feelings out to and it wouldn't judge me and it wouldn't have to understand because it's a dog.

Sometimes I don't take part in activities because I feel like I'm a party pooper. I used to cancel on my friends and tell them my parents said I couldn't hang out and I'd make up some excuse. I love people; I just don't love myself. I write sad stories and try to make up a happy ending but fail and I just steal other people's endings and the story becomes cliché. That's why I am never satisfied with my writing. Sometimes I feel like I owe the whole world an explanation as to why I'm so messed up.

I hate myself because I have to defend myself for being Black and I don't see white people having to defend themselves. A lot of people ask me for the n-word pass. I hate my hair sometimes because people need me to explain and I started shaving my legs to be comfortable wearing dresses. I wanted a nose ring to help accessorize my nose to make it look less ugly. I have been told to lose weight. I built a dam to store all the emotions but I guess it broke down and a massive flood of emotions came out, attacking me. I don't want to be on antidepressants because it gives people another reason to look at me differently besides being Black, besides my weight and besides the scars on my wrist. I feel I have to explain everything to everyone but I don't want pity because that makes me feel weak and different. Everything I do, I think it through and I have a reason for doing it. I don't do things without thinking. Sometimes I get frustrated with knowing that I can't control some things like poverty and hunger, like other kids being harassed, like other suicides and kidney failure deaths, etc. I have hurt a lot of guys and girls, because I only dated them for my own benefit. I dated them to feel loved and complete because at home I never felt loved, because I felt like I couldn't talk to anyone and I would get into trouble for things I didn't do.

You blamed my friends for my state and my friends blamed you and assumptions were constantly made, and it isn't anyone's fault but mine how messed up my life is, but this extra negativity at school and home just made me feel worse. I didn't want my friends coming over because it's like putting a cat and mouse in the same room, but things were getting better and I thought maybe a sleepover would be fun. But then you started blaming Elaine and Austin for my problems and I just said maybe I shouldn't have friends. So I stopped talking to Elaine as often, and I closed up. I prefer staying in my room alone.

And about the guy who has an account just to make people miserable, he said stuff to me, Natasha, my friend Clara, Michel and this random girl. I wanted to do something about it but I can't control it. This person sometimes pretends to be you and hurts other people. He pretended to be Clara and she got suspended because of that. As for me, he says really mean stuff about my weight—you know about that. I get frustrated because of the things I can stop or control and they make me feel powerless and weak.

Right now the medication doesn't make me feel anything but sick, but it's said the effects start showing after two weeks. Before the medication I overthought things at night and I thought of ways I could kill myself. When I heard my phone go off at night, I would read on Quora and give advice to others till I fell asleep.

A lot of people have asked me for pictures of my body and I know how to handle that. I know how to identify a pedophile, and when you and Dad said my Icelandic friend was one and that I couldn't talk to him anymore, I got angry because he was one of the people I could be comfortable with. I helped him feel better about himself, too. His brother died from kidney failure, his mom has kidney failure and his dad is a drunk. I helped him cope with it. My ex, who is two years younger than me, has depression, too, and I helped him cope, as well. The girl he cheated on me with also has depression and I helped her and I talked to her. Other people at school were against her just because she cut her wrist.

One of my guy friends has a father who abandoned him and I helped him cope. He tells me I keep it confidential and I'm not a therapist but therapists suck at their jobs. If I were to talk to a therapist about everything, they would say to delete social media but that is not solving the problem. I help others with relationship advice like how they are drawn to toxic relationships and people who get angry or upset with breakups. I tell them they shouldn't worry about what others think of them because they are worth more than that and don't need a guy/girl to prove it. I tell them that they need themselves only and I advise them not to go straight into another relationship, at least not now, because that's basically asking to get hurt.

There were so many incidents where I had to convince people not to kill themselves and, for me, it's not overwhelming because if I can't help myself, maybe I can help other people. Elaine doesn't show her true emotions and she also has a hard time herself. One of my best friends' mom used to abuse her and she feels trapped and like no one accepts her for who she is and she is not allowed to do a lot of things. My other best friend fakes her emotions. My acquaintance's dad abandoned her. So when you guys tell me that there are other kids going through a lot, I know. I know very well that I'm not the only one feeling like this. But you telling me this makes me think that I'm selfish, and because I already think I'm selfish it doesn't help to hear that.

I didn't write much of a suicide note because I didn't care and nobody else did. I thought why waste my time and plus it's stupid and cliché. Sending this is really hard, so I don't want to talk about it after, and I don't want hugs because that's pity and I hate pity. I want things because I've worked for them, not out of pity. I wrote this letter so that I could make myself clear and so I won't be blamed—like the first time I took the sleeping pills was because I couldn't sleep and I didn't take them ever again, or when I stole candy for my friends when I was young I listened to you the first time when you said that I should ask and I didn't do it again. I hate being blamed for things I didn't do. Before we moved, when the class prefect's title was removed, everyone blamed it on me and I didn't do anything.

Explanation (Version II)

I don't say or talk about how I feel most of the time because the first time I was admitted to the hospital I was lonely. When I was released, I isolated myself because I was scared that I was burdening my friends. Because I pulled away, my friends turned against me and said that I was using depression as an excuse. So I stopped talking about my feelings because in other people's eyes, it was just excuses. When I moved from that horrible place I talked about my feelings to my friends and they were there to listen and that's what friends do. I started to put on a fake face because I didn't want everyone knowing. I later met a guy on the Internet and became friends with him; some of my friends flipped on me and used my depression against me and we stopped talking because of what they did.

I got into a lot of toxic relationships and when they hurt me, I just brushed it off. I can't help but forgive and let people in easily. As for my friends, I forgave them, but we are not as close as we used to be. My friends and I planned to go to the same high school and then move to Norway together and visit on holidays, and possibly our families could celebrate holidays together, but all that went down the drain. One of my friends was consistently there for me. I never told my parents about my problems because I wanted to be independent. I know I won't be able to depend on my parents in the future and that scares me. My parents used to fight bullies for me but I have to learn how to do it myself.

Sometimes I think maybe I should live in the streets and learn how to be a real person with real, hard work to do, not simple chores like dishes and cooking. I want to study culinary arts in university. I didn't say anything to my parents before, because they had high hopes that I would become a doctor or a writer. Sometimes I get really discouraged and I question my worth. Sometimes when I cook, I feel like I'm failing; sometimes I don't eat the food I cook because I feel like it's not going to be good enough.

When I was harassed by the old man, I kept trying to rebuild my self-esteem by requesting to wear tube tops and short skirts, but that was hard. I felt like I needed to do this alone because what if I didn't have parents. I wish I had one of those mother-daughter relationships on Instagram but I don't think I would ever have that because of my mood swings.

I'm an overthinker. It's hard for me to sleep because I overthink things. Sometimes I close my eyes to try to sleep, but then I just start thinking about how to make my life less miserable and more organized and I write those things down but then I lose hope. The boys at my school made me miserable but I hid how I felt because if I showed that I care I would feel weak and hopeless and like I can't feel like that because that would just add one more reason to why living is pointless.

I question life and the point of it all. I get into deep thought about faith and why scientists don't believe in it, because scientists are right about most of the things they discover. Sometimes I think that we are being mind-controlled and sometimes I worry that I'm psychotic and should be institutionalized. I get paranoid in the dark because I feel like my depression is going to drag me to my death. That's why I keep all the lights on in my room. I don't like being outside at night because I'm scared that because of my body I'm going to get myself raped.

The worst feeling is being surrounded by people who love you but still feeling alone and unloved. I distribute love and never get the same amount back but that doesn't bother me that much because I'm mostly focused on my body and other insecurities. When I told my parents that I didn't mind them not being at my basketball games, it was not to guilt-trip them but it was because I got bad anxiety attacks before playing. While playing, though, I stopped thinking too much, which is why I love basketball.

I don't talk about my anxiety because no one would understand and people would just say, "Sleep on it," or "Tomorrow will be better," or "That's life." People say, "I'm here for you," but they are not and it's not comforting whatsoever, and people only say it because it's what the doctors say helps. I say, why bother explaining when no one will ever understand?

I used to cut my arm to get a little bit of control over what I felt because I felt out of control. I didn't do it to be sent to the hospital. I hated being there. It made me feel more alone than ever, and trapped. Alcohol helped me numb the feeling, emotionally and mentally, and I was kind of hoping that I'd get so wasted that I would get the guts to actually end my life. Weed helped me calm down. I used to want a dog and I still do because I read that dogs help support you emotionally, and it would be like a friend who I could pour my feelings out to and it wouldn't judge me and it wouldn't have to understand because it's a dog.

Sometimes don't take part in activities because I feel like I am a party pooper. I used to cancel hanging out with my friends and tell them my parents said I couldn't or make up some excuse. I love people; I just don't love myself that much. I wrote and still write sad stories. I used to try to make up happy endings but I would fail and I'd just end up stealing other people's endings, and then the stories became cliché. That's why I was never satisfied with my writing. I hated myself because I had to defend myself for being Black, and I don't see white people having to defend themselves. A lot of people asked and still do ask me for the n-word pass. I hated my hair because people needed me to explain and I started to shave my legs to be comfortable wearing dresses. I wanted a nose ring to help accessorize my nose to make it look less ugly, and I still want one. I had been told to lose weight, but you know what I did: I just built a dam to store all the emotions, but it eventually broke down and a massive flood of emotions came pouring out, attacking me.

I didn't want antidepressants because I felt like that would just give people another reason to look at me differently besides being Black, besides my weight and besides the scars on my wrist. Now I just keep the antidepressants to myself and hope no one finds out. I feel I have to explain myself all the time, but I don't want pity because that makes me feel weak and different. Everything I do or did, I thought it through and I have reasons for doing it. I don't do things without thinking.

Sometimes I get frustrated with knowing that I can't control somethings like poverty and hunger, like other kids being harassed, like other suicides and kidney failure deaths, etc. I have hurt a lot of guys and girls, because I only dated them for my own benefit. I dated them to feel loved and complete because at home I never felt loved and because I felt like I could not talk to anyone and I would get in trouble for things I didn't do. My parents blamed my friends for my state and my friends blamed my parents and assumptions were constantly made, and it wasn't anyone's fault but mine how messed up my life was, but the extra negativity at school and home just made me feel worse.

I didn't want my friends coming over to my house because it was like putting a cat and mouse in the same room. Eventually, things started getting better and I thought maybe I should have a sleepover. But then the blaming continued and I just said maybe I shouldn't have friends. So I stopped talking to my friends, and I closed up. I prefer staying in my room alone. I got frustrated because of the things I couldn't stop or control and they made me feel powerless and weak. Before the medication I would overthink things at night and I thought of ways I could kill myself. When I had my phone at night, I would read on Quora and give advice to others till I fell asleep. A lot of people asked me for pictures of my body and they still do, but I know how to handle it. I know how to identify a pedophile. When my parents found out about my Internet friend, they said he was a pedophile and that I couldn't talk to him anymore. I got angry because he was one of the only people I was comfortable with. I helped him feel better about himself and I helped him cope with his depression.

A lot of my friends have depression or family problems and I helped them and still help them cope. It is funny how I can help other people cope but I can't even cope myself. I'm not a therapist, but to be honest, therapists suck at their jobs. If I told my therapist about the cyberbullying, she would tell me to delete social media but that wouldn't solve the problem. I helped others with relationship advice, like how they were drawn to toxic relationships and people who got angry or upset with breakups. I told them that they shouldn't worry what anyone else thinks of them because they are worth a lot and they don't need a guy/girl to show them that. I told them that they needed themselves only, and I advised them to not get into a relationship right away because that's basically asking to get hurt.

There were so many incidents where I had to convince people not to kill themselves and, for me, it's not overwhelming because if I can't help myself, maybe I can at least help other people. Some of my friends don't show their true emotions. One of my friends was abused by her mom and she felt useless and like no one accepted her for who she was. My other friend's dad abandoned her, so when I open up to people and they tell me that there are other kids who are going through a lot worse, I know that. I know very well that I'm not the only one feeling empty or oppressed. But people who told me this made me feel like I was being selfish. I mean, I already thought I was selfish but them saying it made me feel horrible.

I didn't write much of a suicide note that day because I didn't care and nobody else did, either, so I thought why waste my time. Plus, I felt it was stupid and cliché. I never regretted that day because I really wanted it to be over, and to be honest, part of me still does want it to be over. But sometimes I feel angry at myself because my grandma felt guilty and felt that it her fault that I tried to kill myself that day. She felt that way because earlier that same day she had told me to loosen up and be nicer to my parents.

Explanation (Version III)

I have been on a journey of ups and downs. This journey was and still is really hard; I have hit so many bumps and, right now, I am facing another one. I have to reach a decision that will impact my whole life. I mean, I had plans, great ones, but I just had to hit this bump.

Decision-making is not my friend. I find it so hard to make decisions, mostly because of my anxiety. I worry too much about the future. When making decisions I don't make them based on how I feel or how they will impact me; I make decisions based on what people I love think I should do—my friends, my parents and the world in general. I feel like I need to explain myself to the world because if I don't, I get super worried about what a person thinks of me. I don't want them to think I'm mentally disabled. To be fair, based on the way I act, I totally seem mentally disabled. Decision-making makes me frustrated, and when I get frustrated I get stressed, and when I'm stressed is when I have a mental breakdown or anxiety attack. I'm afraid if I make one wrong decision it will ruin everything and then I will be a complete failure.

Decision-making is one of the reasons I took becoming a doctor off my list of goals. Doctors have to make decisions life-or-death decisions all the time. I honestly think that doctors are superheroes. Doctors make decisions every single day and even if the outcome is not what they hoped, they don't let themselves get too discouraged. Well, I am the opposite of that because when I fail at something I feel like crap. I feel like I'm not capable of succeeding, it's pointless, I am worthless and will never make it. I'm not a very positive person. I wasn't born with a positive attitude where I see rainbows and sunshine. I had beliefs and hopes but I stopped believing in those when I became a teenager. I used to believe that unicorns were real, I believed I was a princess, I believed in a treasure chest always being at the end of the rainbow, and, mostly, I believed in God. Now, I don't. Princesses are the popular mean girls in middle school, rainbows don't come out often and science destroyed the treasure-chest belief. Unicorns are just pretty horses, and God is something we're told is real so that we feel like there is some meaning to life.

Ever since I was young I was told if you lie, steal, murder and commit other "unholy" crimes, you will go to hell. Here is the thing: every second of every day someone is murdered; everyone has stolen something at least once in their life, and everyone constantly lies. I'm not writing this to prove that life is meaningless and everyone should just die, I'm just saying all the things I believed in when I was younger were taken away, either by science, logic or life in general.

One thing I hate the most is when someone in a relationship leads you on. They say they love you and make empty promises. "Oh, I will never leave you, babe"; "You are my one and only"; "I promise to never leave you." It's so simple: If you don't love someone, don't make empty promises, and if you end up losing feelings for them, don't lead them on just to break up with them in the end.

What is love? Love is a misused word that people constantly throw around like a beach ball. Yes, you may like hearing that you are loved, but what does it really mean to be loved? Love sure doesn't mean you come into my life and make fake promises and then leave. Love requires effort; love comes in different forms. The most important love is the one you have for yourself. Before you commit to or tell someone you love them, you have to ask yourself if you love yourself, because if you don't, your partner won't be able to love you, either. And if you do and actually love your partner, you must give them the love you have for yourself but you must not lose it, because if your partner ends up being a jerk then you must not feel worthless or like you will never be loved.

I personally don't think I will ever be in a relationship, mostly because I lack self-love and I see no point. For me, love is just begging to get hurt but that's just my opinion. I'm super young and I probably don't know what I'm talking about, LOL, but I think I have been in love before, although it didn't work out. But I love my family and my friends; in fact, I consider my friends part of my family.

Do you ever feel frozen? Like you mentally can't operate? It's simple. There's a time when you're feeling demoralized or degraded and when you feel that way, it's as if you are frozen and lost—you can still physically operate but your mind just gives up and becomes inattentive. This is not a condition as such, but it's what you can feel when you are tired of fighting.

I feel frozen all the time. I feel like I'm stuck in my own quantum zone. A quantum zone is like a jail in Marvel movies, in which the villains are trapped. I'm not saying I'm a villain, I'm just saying I feel trapped. Trapped in my own head with a stream of endless, swimming thoughts. My thoughts can be as random as what I want to eat. I'm an overthinker, so it's very easy for me to be trapped in thought.

James Baldwin said, "People are trapped in history and history is trapped in them." I always think about the past and what I could have done differently; I feel haunted by the past. Boys will boys! Why is that? Why is it that boys get away with things with that one phrase while girls are criticized and shamed? Some boys don't know how to behave—yeah, maybe because of peer pressure they are forced to behave some type of way but that's no excuse.

There was this day when I was taking out the trash and this old guy started making comments about my body and what he wanted to do to me. I was petrified but I didn't show fear because if I did, I was scared he would have grabbed me, put me into his car and harmed me. That day remains in my head every day. It was traumatizing, mostly because he was old. I *informed some people but they just said, "Boys will be boys." Thing is, this wasn't a boy, it was a grown man and he could have been a predator but they shrugged it off. People should be more concerned about these types of things. Because, sure, it happened a long time ago so it's history, but it still haunts me. For a while I wore baggy clothes and stayed inside and kept it to myself just so I wouldn't be slut-shamed. It's only after I was in the ER that I decided to tell people what happened, but still they shrugged it off. This kind of commentary by guys (men) makes people insecure and it's the worst feeling. Because of that day I am still insecure about my body. Speaking of insecurities, let's address cyberbullying. There was a day when this random person made some comments on Instagram about my appearance. He called me ugly, and I wasn't going to let it go because I had to stand up for myself. So I asked him why he would say that and he just said, "Because you're ugly," and I replied, "Is there anything else you have to say about me?" Because his big mouth sure had a lot to say. He said, "You should try being vegetarian because you have to lose some weight." This random stranger had the audacity to body-shame me. I was pretty pissed, so I told my cousin about it and he called her a rat. I asked him why he does this to people because I saw that he always posts about other people and criticizes them. I told him he could lead someone to commit suicide. Guess what he said? He said, "I hope I do." I could already tell that he was just a neglected person who wanted attention. I told my aunt about him because I felt like someone should do something about it. The guy could put someone in serious danger because of his words. Words hurt. I talked to my friends about him and warned them that he could be mentally unstable and that he clearly didn't care about people. Some of my friends showed me proof of how they got suspended from school because of him. Apparently, he pretends to be other people and gets them in trouble.*

Cyberbullying is just so low and cold. People who bully others online would never have the guts to say the same things to their face. I feel like if you have a mean opinion about someone you should just keep it to yourself. I once bullied someone. This person used to be my crush and he spread rumours about me at school, so I posted mean things about him. I said if there was a plague, I hoped he would get sick; I said if we had one hour to kill someone, I would go after him first. The guy was a year younger than me. People said he was a cheater and he admitted it, too. I once kicked him in the back because he tried to hit me with a basketball. I was so mean and I didn't know what I was doing, I just felt good since I had been bullied my whole life and I could get revenge. Before he started spreading rumours about me, we were good friends and we had a lot of memories. When I realized what I was doing, I felt so bad. I felt like I was evil. Just because he called me a witch, I called him a plague, but I secretly felt that he was right to call me a witch because I was so cruel. I made him an apology gift and wrote him a letter, but it was not enough— especially after everything I had said. Bullying is bad. Any type of bullying is terrible.

Now for the reason I was in the ER. I just thought you deserved an explanation as to why my life was and maybe still is so messed up. I don't know where to start. It's like a whole long list of things that bother me; sometimes I don't even know how to explain how I feel or felt. I don't know, I just feel like I owe the world an explanation, because if I don't explain myself I get criticized and people assume certain things about me that aren't true. I don't say or talk about how I feel most of the time because the first time I was admitted to the hospital I was very lonely. When I was released, I isolated myself because I was scared that by talking to other people about my problems, I would be burdening them. But because I pulled away, my friends turned against me and said that I was using depression as an excuse. So, I stopped talking about my feelings because in other people's eyes it was all just excuses.

When I moved from Lacombe, I talked about my feelings to my friends and they were there to listen and that's what friends do. I started to put on a fake face because I didn't want everyone knowing how I was really feeling. I met a guy on the Internet and became friends with him, and some of my friends flipped on me and used my depression against me and we stopped talking because of what they did. I got into a lot of toxic relationships and *when they hurt me, I brushed it off. I can't help but forgive and let people in easily. As for my friends, I forgave them, but we're not as close as we used to be. My friends and I planned to go to the same high school and then move to Norway together and visit on holidays and possibly our families could celebrate holidays together, but all that went down the drain.*

One of my friends was there for me. I never told my parents how I was feeling because I wanted to be independent. I know that I won't be able to depend on my parents forever, and that scares me. My parents used to fight my bullies for me but I have to learn how to do it myself. Sometimes I think maybe I should live in the streets and learn how to be a real person with real, hard work to do, not simple chores like dishes and cooking. I want to study culinary arts in university, I didn't say anything to my parents before, because they had high hopes that I would become a doctor or a writer.

Sometimes I get really discouraged and I question my worth. Sometimes when I cook, I feel like I'm failing, and sometimes I don't eat the food I cook because I feel like it's not going to be good enough.

After I was harassed by the old man, I kept trying to rebuild my self-esteem by requesting to wear tube tops and short skirts, but that was hard. I felt like I needed to do this alone because what if I didn't have parents? I wish I had one of those mother-daughter relationships on Instagram, but I don't think I could ever have that because of my mood swings.

I'm an overthinker. It's hard for me to sleep because I overthink things. Sometimes I close my eyes to try to sleep, but then I just start thinking about how to make my life less miserable and more organized and I write those things down but then I lose hope. The boys at my school made me miserable but I hid how I felt because if I showed that I care, I would feel weak and hopeless and like I can't feel like that because that would just add one more reason to why living is pointless.

I question life and the point of it all. I get into deep thought about faith and why scientists don't believe in it, because scientists are right about most of the things they discover. Sometimes I think that we are being mind-controlled, and sometimes I worry that I'm psychotic and should be institutionalized, I get paranoid in the dark because I feel like my depression is going to drag me to my death. That's why I leave all the lights on in my room. I don't like being outside at night because I'm scared that because of my body I'm going to get myself raped.

The worst feeling is being surrounded by people who love you but still feeling alone and unloved. I distribute love and never get the same amount back but that doesn't bother me that much because I'm mostly focused on my body and other insecurities. When I told my parents that I didn't mind them not being at my basketball games, it was not to guilt-trip them but it was because I got bad anxiety attacks before playing. While playing, though, I stopped thinking too much, which is why I love basketball.

I don't talk about my anxiety because no one would understand and people would just say, "Sleep on it," or "Tomorrow will be better," or "That's life." People say, "I'm here for you," but they are not and it's not comforting whatsoever, and people only say it because it's what the doctors say helps. I say, why bother explaining when no one will ever understand?

I used to cut my arm to get a little bit of control over what I felt because I felt out of control. I didn't do it to be sent to the hospital. I hated being there. It made me feel more alone than ever, and trapped. Alcohol helped me numb the feeling, emotionally and mentally, and I was kind of hoping that I'd get so wasted that I would get the guts to actually end my life. Weed helped me calm down. I used to want a dog and I still do because I read that dogs help support you emotionally, and it would be like a friend who I could pour my feelings out to and it wouldn't judge me and it wouldn't have to understand because it's a dog.

Sometimes I wouldn't take part in activities because I felt like I was a party pooper, I used to cancel hanging out with my friends and tell them my parents said I couldn't or make up some excuse. I love people; I just don't love myself that much. I wrote and still write sad stories. I used to try to make up happy endings but I would fail and I would just end up stealing other people's endings, and then the stories became cliché. That's why I was never satisfied with my writing. I hated myself because I had to defend myself for being Black and I don't see white people having to defend themselves. A lot of people asked and still do ask me for the n-word pass. I hated my hair because people needed me to explain, and I started to shave my legs to be comfortable wearing dresses. I wanted a nose ring to help accessorize my nose to make it look less ugly, and I still want one. I had been told to lose weight but you know what I did: I just built a dam to store all the emotions, but it eventually broke down and a massive flood of emotions came pouring out, attacking me.

I didn't want antidepressants because I felt like that would just give people another reason to look at me differently besides being Black, besides my weight and besides the scars on my wrist. Now I just keep the antidepressants to myself and hope no one finds out. I feel I have to explain myself all the time, but I don't want pity because that makes me feel weak and different. Everything I do or did, I thought it through, and I had reasons for doing it. I don't do things without thinking. Sometimes I get frustrated with knowing that I can't control somethings like poverty and hunger, like other kids being harassed, like other suicides and kidney failure deaths, etc. I've hurt a lot of guys and girls, because I only dated them for my own benefit. I dated them to feel loved and complete, because at home I never felt loved and because I felt like I couldn't talk to anyone and would get in trouble for things I didn't do. My parents blamed my friends for my state and my friends blamed my parents and assumptions were constantly made, and it wasn't anyone's fault but mine how messed up my life was or is, but the extra negativity at school and home just made me feel worse.

I didn't want my friends coming over to my house because it was like putting a cat and mouse in the same room. Eventually, things started getting better and I thought maybe I should have a sleepover. That's what I thought. But then the blaming continued and I just said maybe I shouldn't have friends. So I stopped talking to my friends, and I closed up. I prefer staying in my room alone. I got frustrated because of the things I couldn't stop or control and they made me feel powerless and weak.

Before the medication, I would overthink things at night and I thought of ways I could kill myself. When I had my phone at night, I would read on Quora and give advice to others till I fell asleep. A lot of people asked me for pictures of my body and they still do, but I know how to handle it. I know how to identify a pedophile. When my parents found out about my Internet friend, they said he was a pedophile and that I couldn't talk to him anymore. I got angry because he was one of the people I was comfortable with. I helped him feel better about himself and I helped him cope with his depression. A lot of my friends have depression or family problems and I helped them and still help them cope. It is funny how I can help other people cope but I can't even cope myself. I'm not a therapist, but to be honest, therapists suck at their jobs. If I told my therapist about the cyberbullying, would tell me to delete social media but that wouldn't solve the problem. I helped others with relationship advice, like how they were drawn to toxic relationships and people who got angry or upset with breakups. I told them that they shouldn't worry about what other people thought of them because they are worth a lot and they don't need a guy/girl to show them that. I told them that they needed themselves only, and I advised them to not get into a relationship right away because that's basically asking to get hurt.

There were so many incidents where I had to convince people not to kill themselves and, for me, it's not overwhelming because I if I can't help myself, maybe I can at least help other people. Some of my friends don't show their true emotions. One of my friends was abused by her mom and she felt useless and like no one accepted her for who she was. My other friend's dad abandoned her. So, when I open up to people and they tell me that there are other kids going through a lot worse, I know that. I know very well that I'm not the only one feeling empty or oppressed. But people who told me this made me feel like I was being selfish. I mean, I already thought I was selfish but them saying it made me feel horrible.

I didn't write much of a suicide note that day because I didn't care and nobody else did, either, so I said why waste my time. Plus, I felt it was stupid and cliché. I never regretted that day because I really wanted it to be over and, to be honest, part of me still does want it to be over. But sometimes I feel angry at myself because my grandma felt guilty and that it her fault that I attempted to kill myself that day. She felt that way because earlier that day, she had told me to loosen up and be nicer to my parents.

I have been in the ER twice so far for trying to kill myself. I'm going to talk about addictions now. I was addicted to cutting and almost got addicted to alcohol and drugs. I craved alcohol so much; I learned to create good combinations, such as Glenfiddich malt whisky and Sprite with a teaspoon of lime juice. I put alcohol in a lot of things I ate or drank. I used to put it in yogurt, coffee, ice cream and lots of other things. I craved it but I could control the cravings. Weed and nicotine were not as bad for me as alcohol because I was mindful about other people's health; even though I wanted to die didn't mean other people did.

The cutting was probably the worst. I used to cut so much I still have the scars. It was better in the shower because I liked seeing the blood drip into the drain. My mother got me Bio-Oil to get rid of the scars but I don't put it on. I love my scars. They are my battle wounds and I want to keep them so I won't forget. They will eventually disappear but I want to keep them until then. Addictions are hard to get over. Sometimes you need help to get over addictions and sometimes you don't. Sometimes you just have to wake yourself up and tell yourself that this is not right. One thing I have learned is that to get to the top of a steep mountain, you have to go through the obstacles.

Three a.m. is the time I feel most trapped in my thoughts and emotions. It feels like being in an endless tunnel with everything that I have bottled up or hidden from everyone. Night is the one time you can take off your mask and let everything out. Although lonely, it is actually the most peaceful and quietest time to be awake. Three a.m. is a dark hour. It's dark, quiet and lonely. Your thoughts stream through your head. You carefully observe every thought, from the happiest thought to the saddest. Night is when most breakdowns happen. It is when you cry silently because you don't want to be heard or wake anyone up. The night can make you go crazy, make you *feel like you're insane but you're not—you're just in so much pain. I used to live in the night, but it's a very horrible place to live in.*

I have recently discovered the word "whitewashed." See, I am Black and I am expected to act Black; it doesn't really make sense but it is what it is. Apparently, I am whitewashed, which means I act white. They say because I like Taylor Swift, I am whitewashed. Ever since I heard that, I've felt out of place around my kind of people because it's like I do not belong anywhere.

After putting it all out there on paper, I was able to enter the acceptance stage. I started hanging out with my best friends more to distract myself, especially Elaine. We would call each other 24/7. Our calls usually lasted for at least one hour. We would go to the skate park and hang out and we made a new friend. This friend was different, but I got along pretty well with her because we were both troublemakers in our own way. She told us about her relationship with her brother, which was an incestuous one. She said that technically he was her step-cousin so it was fine to be sleeping with him and dating him. I celebrated my birthday with Elaine and got my licence in May. In June, Elaine, Kim, Amanda and I celebrated Em's birthday with her, even though it was raining. I got stuck inside the skate park and couldn't climb back up, but my friends eventually helped me get out. We saw a deer and ate pizza. When I got home, I was soaked but happy. It was during this time that I started writing stories, knitting and generally being more productive, due in large part to the quarantine imposed by Covid-19. I've included some of the stories and essays I wrote over the next several pages.

COVID-19

Lockdown Diary #1

People make living harder than it should be. There could be peace and less homelessness if only people didn't make living so hard. On Saturday, I was talking to my mom about homeless people. I asked my mom if she had money to give a homeless person we saw and she said no. What she said was "I'd rather donate to the church than to homeless people because the homeless guy might be a drug addict and I would just be supporting his habit." She was scared that the drugs would be the reason the homeless guy would end up dying, and she would have contributed to his death by giving him money to buy them. I gave her my point of view and it was that she didn't know if he was a drug addict or a criminal and giving him five bucks wouldn't be enough to buy him drugs anyway; she didn't know the reason he was homeless, and she could at least give him some money to buy blankets, food and water. He could die from drugs or he could die from hunger; as long as her heart was in the right place, if he died, it wouldn't be on her, it would be on him.

Afterwards, my mom asked, "Say that someone stole some money and the two suspects were a priest and a criminal who'd been to jail before. Who would you think did it?" and I said it would be fifty-fifty because just because someone committed a crime in the past doesn't mean you can assume they committed the crime, and just because priests are generally considered to have high morals doesn't mean that they should be treated any differently than any other person.

Lockdown Diary #2

Do you ever feel frozen, like you mentally cannot operate? At times that you feel demoralized or degraded you might feel that way—you can still physically operate but your mind just gives up and tunes out. This is not a condition as such, but it's what you can feel when you are tired of fighting.

I started feeling like this a month ago, I used to fight against this feeling but now I just accept it. If you told me something that I needed to remember, I probably wouldn't remember, not because I have memory loss but because I'm just unaware; I've stopped paying attention. I won't be daydreaming or anything, but I mentally disappear and I call it being frozen.

My name is Candy, I'm 15 years old and I live in Norway. I am originally from Tokyo, Japan. I moved here two years ago in 2017 when my stepbrother was born. I live with my stepmother, my stepfather and stepbrother. How does that work, you ask? Well, my dad abandoned me when I was younger and my mom got married; she died because of cancer and my stepdad remarried and I don't have other relatives who could take me in. The way I explained how my mom died might sound cold, but I honestly don't care because she was abusive whenever my stepdad wasn't there, so I'm kind of relieved she's gone

My stepdad, Austin Yanders, was always kind to me and kind enough to take me in; as for my stepmom, Yolanda Yanders, she loves me the same way she loves my stepbrother, Noah, who is seven years old. Noah and I also love each other.

You're probably wondering why I'm ranting right now. Well, first off, I'm not wanted. I was never wanted and never will be. Knowing that my biological dad is out there somewhere in the world, breaking hearts just like he broke mine and my mom's makes me so upset. My mom would sometimes hit me for no reason but I honestly understand why. My mom, Marshy Knowles, was depressed, and hitting me was a release for her. It is a bad coping mechanism but it does make sense.

My mother had Noah with my stepdad, so he is technically my stepbrother. So, the reason I am complaining about my life is because of what happened a month ago on my birthday. My birthday is on the 17th of March. I woke up on my birthday and I saw Austin and Yolanda beside my bed. They sang "Happy Birthday" to me. I wasn't really surprised because they do it every year. Yolanda buys my favourite cake, a French vanilla coffee-flavoured cake, and lights up a candle for me to blow out. Yolanda and Austin are really kind to me. My birthday isn't something I typically like to celebrate because I've always felt like I was a mistake and that I wasn't good enough and that that is why my biological parents left me.

Nothing extraordinary usually happens on my birthday, but this time it was different. See, I share a birthday with Camilla, a girl from my school who is also my neighbour and is really popular and doesn't like me. I am jealous of Camilla because she has two parents who love her. This year Camilla got a pink Chevy for her birthday and she was having her sweet sixteen party at her house. Yolanda and Austin wanted to throw a party for me but I said no because Camilla would be really pissed. Noah hates Camilla's little sister, Ava, because she had a crush on him, but I secretly think maybe in future they will end up together.

Anyway, the thing that made my birthday different this year was my dad. I officially turned 16 at 9:00 p.m., so that's when I could eat cake—that's Yolanda's tradition. So, that night on my birthday I watched movies with the family and waited for 9:00 p.m. to eat the cake. Finally it was nine, and we cut the cake and then we heard a knock. I went to the door and opened it and you would never guess who I saw standing there. It was my dad. I dropped down and started crying. He was wearing a white suit and holding the same cake we were about to eat.

I said, "What are you doing here?" in a soft, sad voice.

He replied, "Candice, I'm so sorry for leaving you."

I never knew why my dad left me because I was six and I didn't understand anything that was going on. So, I asked him why he left and he told me the truth. My dad left because of my mother; they divorced and she filed a restraining order against him because my dad wanted to take me away from her. She framed him for abusing me, when it was really my mom who was abusive. I was six and she hit me and blamed it on my dad. I asked my dad why she would want to keep me just to hurt me, and he told me that my mom was psychotic. It hurt me to hear the truth but at least now I know.

I also asked my dad why he didn't come back for me two years ago when my mom died, and he told me that he was in rehab and coming back at that time wouldn't have been a good idea. I felt frozen after I heard the truth and it took me time to process everything that happened, but after a month I moved in with my dad and my story changed. I am no longer a sad and lonely girl. I have my dad.

Hi, my name is Candice Miller. I'm 16 years old. I live with my beloved dad, Caiden Miller, in a big, modern house. Ever since I was reunited with my dad, I have never felt frozen or incomplete. My dad is my best friend and I'm so happy around him. As for the Yanders family, we always visit and we spend Thanksgiving and other holidays together.

Lockdown Diary #3

I wish I was like most girls. Most girls are really pretty and they have amazing hair, they get good grades, they are cheerleaders, they play volleyball and they are just so perfect. I am not perfect. My name is April. I am from Australia and I am 14 years old. I have sapphire blue eyes and my hair is a natural blueish-purple pastel colour. I technically live alone because my parents are lawyers and they work from 3 a.m. to 2 a.m. The only day my parents don't work is Mondays and every Monday I have an eye appointment because my eyes are peculiar, so they try to figure out what is wrong with my eyes from 6 to 9 p.m., which is immediately after school, and then my parents go to bed because they have to work the next day. I don't have any siblings, so it is kind of lonely. I may be rich but I'm weird and different. My parents say that I am unique, but unique is a way to hide being weird and peculiar. I am ugly and I don't even know how to put makeup on. Other girls wear nice dresses and shorts but I wear baggy hoodies and sweatpants. Other girls have perfect bodies and I look like a potato. Most girls have normal eyes and hair and I have weird-looking eyes and my hair doesn't look real. People say things like, "You're damaging your hair by dyeing it," or "Why do you wear contacts? You might go blind." The thing is I have never dyed my hair and if I did dye my hair, I would lose my hair and I don't wear contacts because I don't even know how to put them in.

I don't have friends at school. I don't let people in because I am a freak and everyone thinks that—or, that's what I thought.

A few weeks ago at school I met a girl named Alora and she is different, too. Alora is the same age as me. She's Black and she has orange hair and eyes like mine. Alora recently moved to Sydney and she is really pretty. She has braces that match her hair and she wears sweatpants and crop tops. She came up to me and we started talking. Alora and I have become really close. Alora lives with her mom who is a pastry chef. Alora told me that I was beautiful and different; she didn't say I was "unique" and she didn't try to make me feel better by trying to cover up the fact that I was not like other girls.

I am April. I love hiking and soccer and I am not like other girls and neither is Alora, but that is perfectly fine.

Lockdown Diary #4

I'm pretty sure everyone has felt at least one of these things: lost, confused, unclear, bewildered, perplexed, disoriented or unsure, because I have, and none of these is a good feeling. The way I overcome these things is through relaxation, meditation and acceptance, but these things were hard for me at first. I couldn't relax because I was frustrated and agitated; I couldn't meditate because I felt suppressed and dejected; I couldn't accept who I was because I was not a person who could accept that there is pain, sorrow and disorientation. But I looked at myself in the mirror, wiped my tears and washed my face and do you know what I asked myself? I asked myself why I was doing this to myself—torturing myself, pulling anxiety in my direction—and guess what my answer was? I don't know. So, I pulled up my socks and meditated for two weeks. I didn't exactly relax but I accepted my situation and moved on. The lesson I learned was not to let my guard down, to accept facts and try to change facts and to know that there are a lot of circumstances in life that we all have to deal with.

Lockdown Diary #5

I was never a skeptical person before. I was honest with myself and I accepted reality easily. What happened? I know what happened: I realized that I was not truthful to myself in the beginning. I was dishonest with myself because I did not accept things easily, and I realized that the moment I set foot in North America.

When I came to Canada, I didn't really feel welcomed; I felt like an outcast. I felt dejected and like I was being crushed in a garlic press, first torn to pieces then pulverized slowly and surely. The worst thing I did was that I didn't do anything about the fact that I was suppressed. Instead, I started judging people like I was a judge on *America's Got*

Talent. I couldn't blame anyone but myself for turning into a selfish person.

Before, I was not perfect, but at least I felt good about myself. The change in me was no one's fault but mine. I allowed my fears to get to me, to the extent that they started to take over my life. I was afraid of change because a little bit of change can decide your fate completely and it can ruin you; the fact that it can change your fate really frightened me. I had to overcome this fear and I got help from two amazing friends. They were nice to me and welcomed me. I was able to complete the first stage of my journey and I was really proud of myself, but I never would have taken that first step without my two friends. The moment these two girls walked up to me to say hi, I knew it was the beginning of a new journey, a fresh start and a new chapter. Sometimes I look back to that day asking myself what if I did not find the courage to face my obstacles or what if my two friends who helped had never helped me open my eyes? My friends tell me I shouldn't think too much about it and I should focus on the present, not the past and most definitely not the future.

It was really hard to accept change and to defeat my insecurities, but I had accomplished the first step to being better. I learned that sometimes you need a little push to achieve greater things; there are always obstacles in the way to success. Everyone is brave and everyone is strong, even the shy ones—you just have to find the brave in you to find the strong you. I found something special in me with help from people I love. People may say that I am not independent because I needed help to make it to where I am today, and I am helpless without others, but no one is ever fully dependent and no one is perfect, either. I reached out for help, which is better than enduring the pain and fear; because I asked for a hand, I became stronger than before.

It takes two to tango. My grandfather always told me that you need someone to walk with you through both the difficult times and the awesome ones.

Lockdown Diary #6

Okay, this is not an essay or anything: I am just expressing my feelings. I express my feelings through writing. I love writing. I LOVE writing. Writing is my first hobby besides dancing. Most dancers express their feelings when they dance, but it's usually when I'm writing that my feelings come out and they come out true. I started writing when I learned how to write. I used to write short stories, but now I write long stories and it helps me let out my emotions. My handwriting is not the best but my writing comes from the heart. I don't know, but writing seems to come to me in a different way than it does for others—at least that's what I think.

I don't know why every time I'm sad I listen to sad songs and start writing, but even if I'm in a loud, noisy place, I can write from my heart and I won't be distracted. I want people to love or have an interest in my writing, but at the same time I don't. At school I write for assignments; otherwise, I write for myself. I have a blog on wordpress.com and I have published a couple of my stories. I sometimes care about how many people view them but I mostly don't care.

I do not like talking about my feelings because they make me sad and cry. I try to talk about them but it's very hard for me to let people in. The only people I can talk to about my feelings are my two best friends because I trust them from the bottom of my heart.

Lockdown Diary #7

I am Heaven Mitchell and I'm 15 years old and I am from Atlanta. I live with my mother, Hope Mitchell, and my father, Dylan Mitchell. I love my family, but I loved my sister, Hope, the most. She was 17 years old and in her last year of high school when I was in tenth grade. I was so bummed that she was going to university in Canada when she could just stay with us here in the US. Every day I tried to convince her to stay here but she always said, "In the US you have to be 21 to drink alcohol, and plus, Trump is here," and I always told her drinking was not important and Trump was going to be replaced soon, but she didn't listen.

Hope and I had the most amazing time when we were kids; she was always there for me. She saved me from falling off a cliff when I was nine and we shared everything. One day my parents had to go to a wine-tasting event in Italy and you know when you are home alone as a teen you like to go a little wild, so after school I brought my two friends, Clara and Lauren, over. Mom said she didn't want me hanging around them because they did bad things like smoking, drinking, drugs and catfishing guys from our school, but I didn't listen to my mom. I still hung out with them.

I went up to my room and my sister was still working, so we had two hours to be rebellious and the first thing we did was put on makeup and borrow my sister's clothes. Then we went shopping with her money. We bought a lot of clothes and then Clara said, "We should get tattoos and piercings," and I said, "The card will get suspended and won't work for a month, and the $10,000 is for my sister's stationery." Then Lauren said, "She's being a wimp, let's not hang out with her anymore." I don't know why I said this, but I did. I said, "Okay, fine, we should. And we should invite Jake, Ben and Owen over to my house after."

So we did. I got a tattoo on my wrist that says, "I'm relevant," and a nose piercing at the right side of my nose; Clara got a belly piercing and a tattoo near her hip that says, "Can't touch this"; and Lauren got a tongue piercing and a tattoo on her knuckles that says, "Fight." Afterwards, we went to my house and the boys had already arrived and were waiting in my room. The boys had brought a bunch of vapes and alcohol; I wasn't allowed any of that but I thought a bit couldn't hurt and we had a lot. Later, my sister came home and saw that we had trashed the house, and she got angry and chased everyone out.

"Heaven Amery Mitchell, what the heck have you done? Piercings, tattoos, alcohol and **VAPES**??? Are you trying to kill yourself?" she screamed.

I replied, "Don't yell! My head hurts so bad."

"No kidding . . . you were **VAPING**," she said. "If Mom and Dad hear about this, they will disown you."

"Are you going to tell?" I asked her.

"No." She sighed. "Just tell me why you did this? You're not like this, Heaven."

"Well, I wanted to be cool so I maxed out your debit card and did all of this," I replied.

"YOU DID WHAT??? Don't you know that was my university money!"

I replied, "I am so sorry."

"I have to tell Mom," she said. "I can't come up with a reason for her to give me $10,000. I'm sorry, but this is now on you."

I screamed, "Hope, NO . . . please don't! I'm sorry!!!"

"Don't yell at me," she said. "This is your fault—you were being a spoiled brat and doing messed-up crap. It's all on you, Heaven. I'm tired of defending you."

I said, "But that's what sisters do, isn't it?"

"Heaven, I can't, okay? You freaking wrecked this place! This is not a little thing like when you tore mom's wedding dress. I can't say that a racoon maxed out my card . . . that would be stupid."

"I hate you for this! Go to hell!" I snapped as I ran out to the frozen lake, balling my eyes out. I stormed through the snowstorm wearing my pajama shorts and a tank top and I couldn't feel the cold. All I was focused on was the fact that my world was going to be wrecked. The thing about people is that the moment you do one horrible thing, they focus on that horrible thing you did, and all the good things you've done in the past are overshadowed by that one bad thing.

As I kept running, my sister was behind me, chasing after me and calling my name. I wondered how she had time to put on her warm clothes and still catch up to me. At that moment, I stopped thinking and I was just gone. I disappeared mentally. I looked down at my yellow

Vans. I took them off because I couldn't bear seeing them anymore because they reminded me of how I maxed out my sister's card. I stepped down onto the snow with my bare feet, and at that moment I didn't care if I got frostbite. I value my parents' trust and respect and I hate to disappoint them.

I finally reached the lake which was two kilometres away, and I ran to the middle of the half-frozen lake so my sister couldn't get me unless she risked her life, too. I sat down and started to cry. My hands and feet were trembling and I could feel that my face was pale. My sister had finally reached the water's edge and she yelled at me. The ice started cracking and she ran to me and carried me and threw me by the edge of the lake and then she fell into the water.

I couldn't breathe. Everything was foggy. I had hit my head so hard that all I could remember was seeing a foggy figure and muffled yelling, and then I immediately collapsed.

I woke up in the hospital and the first thing I saw was a blood drip. Apparently when I hit my head, I lost a lot of blood and went into a concussion. I lay there, confused, and then my parents came into my ward and they were in tears. I could tell that they were really sad and I asked, "What's wrong, Mom?" and my dad looked infuriated and he said in an anger-filled voice, "What do you think is wrong, huh? You killed your sister!" Then my mom interrupted him. "Honey, watch your tone," she said and her voice sounded soft.

The doctor then came in and explained what had happened and I teared up. My sister was dead. He said she had hypothermia. My dad was right: it was all my fault.

When I went back home nothing was the same. I got so depressed and therapy didn't help. I miss her so much. She was always there for me and I was so selfish. I am filled with remorse and regret. After everything that happened, I have learned to be unpretentious and selfless. I have to face the fact that my sister is gone and I have to somehow move on—and that is what I'm going to do.

THE LOCKDOWN EXPERIENCE

Lockdown was really hard but it gave everyone time to grow and learn new things. In July, my brother and I went to Fort McMurray for the rest of the summer. We had fun but I had I started talking to someone who happened to live in Fort McMurray. It wasn't anything serious at first; we were just really great friends. We called each other a couple of times and texted a lot. I'm going to call him "Flexing Star" here, because he used to flex so much—his confidence was unbelievable. It wasn't the type of confidence where someone is cocky, conceited and selfish; rather, he was unpretentious, modest and selfless. He didn't talk about himself like crazy. On the phone we talked about our childhood and how everyone called me whitewashed just because I like Taylor Swift. We talked about music and dead legends. He was open and honest with me about everything but his age and his relationship status.

Before I explain how I found out that he was lying to me, I'm going to explain how our relationship progressed to a higher spot in the relationship hierarchy. My brother and I had to leave Fort McMurray early because one of our family members got Covid. When we were back in Red Deer was when I started talking to Flexing Star even more. I remember talking to Elaine about him so much—then he finally asked me to be his girlfriend. Technically, I asked him by a TikTok trend; he saw right through it and asked me to be his girlfriend. I obviously said yes because I really liked him.

One day, we played a question game to get to know each other better. I told him one of my many talents was twerking. Because I'm African, I grew up watching family members and other people twerk and I learned from them. He doubted that a whitewashed 14-year-old would be any good at twerking and he asked for proof. I sent him an old video that I posted on TikTok and he said I wasn't bad. As more time passed, he asked for more twerking videos and I sent them to him. I trusted him because they were not vulgar and they were already posted on my TikTok account anyway.

Another day, we played Truth or Dare around one a.m. because we both couldn't sleep and it got dirty. He asked me to send him naked pictures of myself, and I said I'd do it only if he did, too. We traded and it became an everyday thing. He liked waking up to a shirtless mirror pic. I never felt uncomfortable sending them to him. Of course, I never wanted them leaked but if Flexing Star wanted to leak them then they would have already been made public as I write this. I eventually stopped sending them because I had a gut feeling about it and a terrible one. He noticed I stopped and he thought I was mad at him for some reason, but I said no, it was just because I was too lazy, and he was respectful about it.

Another day I was angry because he wasn't talking to me that much anymore, so when he texted I ignored it and when he called, I ignored that too. I eventually answered and I said, "What do you want? Nothing? Thought so, bye!!!" and hung up. He kept calling me and then I answered again and he asked what was wrong and I said nothing. He showed so much concern and it was cute how worried he was. He then said if I didn't want to tell him what was up we could talk about other stuff. I don't remember what we talked about because I was just focused on how much I was smiling and the butterflies that were in my stomach. I do remember him talking to my brother and it was the cutest conversation ever and my brother said, "I'm going to tell Mom you have a husband," and we laughed so much—and then I blackmailed him into not saying anything. Flexing Star started talking about the four-letter word. He had asked if it was too early to say it and I said of course it was, and that it had to be said in person.

So, because it needed to be said in person, we started making plans to meet. I knew Red Deer like the back of my hand, so I knew how to meet him without raising suspicion or getting in trouble. We were going to go to the mall and because he was 17, he could drive, and we could go to the lake to go swimming. He also wanted to sleep with me and I said that would be okay if he used protection. If I had been who I was before I started dating the Icelandic guy back in February, I would have said hell no, but I felt I was ready.

In all honesty, if I was not insecure about my body, my body count would be so high. I don't know how other teenagers view sex, but for me I think that it's like a sport. It's a sport to see how much you can endure. One thing I know is that intercourse is not a must in a relationship. There is pleasure that comes with the sport but it seems to be more of a last-man-standing game—if you think about it, there is always a winner and a loser.

So, anyway, Flexing Star was going to drive from Fort McMurray to Red Deer to spend time with me. A few days before he was coming, I was bored and I wanted to talk to him but he was busy and I got worried and thought that he was trying to make me jealous by saying he was going to watch *Kissing Booth II* with a Latina girl. I checked his location on my phone and he wasn't where he said he was going. I let it slide and I decided to google him to watch his football highlights again, and I came across a picture of him with another girl. I thought it was his sister at first, but then I saw that they had different last names. I tried to make myself believe that it was his cousin, but I couldn't. The girl was friends with my 20-year-old cousin's friend, so I went on a family group chat to ask about him.

That's how I found out Mr. Perfect was actually 20 years old and was dating someone else. If it was only the age, I wouldn't have overreacted but he was also seeing another girl. I cried because she was Latina and way prettier and smarter than me. When I confronted Flexing Star, he blocked me. My cousins kept asking questions and some even wanted to go and jump him. I got anxious because they were talking about involving the cops. I emailed my therapist because I was so anxious I couldn't breathe. I eventually calmed down and went to bed, but when I woke up my therapist had called. I called her back and she said she had to inform the authorities and my parents.

Out of fear, I took off on my bike. I rode to the highway with a pocket knife for self-defence. I was sitting there, wondering what I should do. Then I made the stupid mistake of telling my therapist I was on the highway, and she assumed I was going to kill myself. The cops found me and took my knife away. I wanted to make a run for it but I knew I wouldn't get far. I ignored the cop when he was talking to me and he handcuffed me and made me get into his car. Then he took me to the hospital.

I didn't care what was happening around me. I was thinking about where I went wrong with Flexing Star. I was admitted to Unit 39 for the second time, but this time I was there for longer. They saw through my faking—usually faking that I learned my lesson would get me out the next day. I had to bring my A-game to fool them this time. I did what I was told, completed my worksheet and worked on a mindful statement so they would think I was improving. Some of what I told them was the truth but the majority of the things I said were lies; eventually, I succeeded in convincing them. While in the hospital, I was called by my therapist and she asked if I wanted to press charges, which was kind of stupid; it is not a good idea to ask a mentally troubled person to make a decision in the hospital. I said yes, not knowing what I was getting myself and Flexing Star into.

I managed to get released in time for the family Banff trip. I was discharged with instructions: I was not allowed to use my phone for three months and after the three months, there would be limitations. I was still taking my antidepressants but I was way worse than before—and when I say worse than before, I honestly got worse. We went to Banff with the whole family, and I was glad to see my cousins and we had a lot of fun. But I still had Flexing Star on my mind and I was going crazy.

When my cousins and I were playing the game, Concentration, after white-water rafting, I said Flexing Star's name and one of my younger cousins asked, "Isn't that the bad guy?" and I asked who told her that and she said her 20-year-old sister had been talking about it. I let it go and moved on. Then, when I was with some of the adults, I overheard them talking about me and my involvement with the male species, which added fuel to my anger, but I also let that slide. The thing that triggered my fight-or-flight the most was what my older cousins said. We were playing with the kids and I said something out of pocket to my male cousin but obviously didn't mean it because we joke around like that. My older cousins were about to go out and they overheard it and one of them said, "You guys can bully each other, but don't involve the parents." It made me so angry because they didn't want us snitching on them for being irresponsible, but they told the adults what I said and let the kids know that I was in a relationship with a quote-unquote "pedophile." They didn't even tell the story right; they made me out to be a weak victim and Flexing Star, a criminal.

When the older cousins came back, the one I'm going to call "Tiffany" because she was the only one I trusted at the moment, talked to the cousin I was mad at. I'm going to call the cousin I was mad at "Brooklyn." While they were talking, I decided to tell all the kids who received false information about me and Flexing Star the truth—my truth. Brooklyn got mad because I told them my truth; she was mad that my truth was so different compared to hers. One thing she didn't understand was that it wasn't her story to tell in the first place and that she had no right to twist the kids' minds and make me seem weak. She wanted to talk to me and I said no, and because I said no, it infuriated her more. She yelled and grabbed my wrists tight. I broke free and went out the door, crying. Tiffany followed and talked to me. She told me what else Brooklyn had been doing behind my back.

Brooklyn came and followed me outside and she made me listen to what she had to say. She told me that she had ridden for me more than any of our cousins and more than even her sisters. She said she didn't tell the kids false information. I believed she was telling the truth because she was crying and she never cries. We started walking back to the hotel and then one of the adults came and grabbed my wrists hard. I put weight on myself and made myself fall to the ground. I started breaking down. I ran into the middle of the road, hoping a car would come hit me. I was crying so hard and the adult who had come after me was threatening to call the police. I kept crying. Brooklyn and her sister told the adult to go back and that they would calm me down.

When I calmed down, we started walking back to the house. My mom came outside and I found out that she was the one who told the adults about what happened and not my cousins. I lost it and I started walking away in tears. I didn't know where I was going but I needed to get away. I ended up going back to get my journal and shoes because I didn't have any shoes on. My dad came out and I told him I didn't want to talk. He yelled at me, saying that he didn't want me, and that made me cry even more.

Brooklyn and her sister took me to their room, and before I went to sleep I cut my wrists. In the middle of the night, I woke up all sweaty and I took my journal and shoes and tried to leave again. Brooklyn's sister saw me and asked me to promise not to leave and that she would convince the adults to take me to Fort McMurray with them.

The next day, we went back to my house. Brooklyn's sister was just like her sister: a liar. I ran away and went to Kim's house, and her mom let me stay for the night. I had to go back home after. When I went back home, I didn't speak to my parents; I kept to myself. I would leave home early in the morning and come back late at night. I stopped taking my antidepressants and I wouldn't eat because I was scared they would put my pills in my food or drinks. I would go to Elaine's house and she would cook and force me to eat because she was scared that I was losing weight. We would go skating and hang out with other friends a lot. When I wasn't hanging out with Elaine, I was hanging out with my older friends, who my parents, if they'd known about them, would call "bad influences." We would smoke and at times I would sleep with them, both girls and boys. I spent most of my time with Elaine, though, because she lived far from Red Deer. Elaine didn't know the people I hung out with when I wasn't with her. Once, I stayed out till midnight and asked a police officer to take me home. The cop said, "We are not a taxi service." When I got home, my parents thought I was under the influence but I wasn't; I hadn't smoked or done any drugs that night.

The good news was my parents agreed that I could go stay in Fort McMurray, but they picked the wrong time to make that decision. In exchange, I agreed I wouldn't cause any trouble, I would take my pills and I would do an interview with the police. I did everything they said I should do just so I could move to Fort McMurray. I stayed with Brooklyn's family, and back then we were on good terms.

I couldn't stop thinking about Flexing Star. I wanted to go and see him and ask him the truth about what happened. I was completely obsessed with him. I was determined to find him and ask if I meant anything to him. I found the address of his college in Montreal. I had the dean's number and a connection to his friend. I talked to his friend and he told me he had said that he cared about me and that he hadn't lied to me about anything but his relationship status and age. I was so happy to hear that he cared about me—although my views on that changed recently . . . I will explain why later.

I started reading a book called *Night Road* by Kristin Hannah and I liked it. I could relate to it so much. I thought about Flexing Star and about how I loved him and wanted him with ferocity. In the book there was a quote I liked: "The stars overhead became their private universe." I thought that maybe things would have been different between Flexing Star and me if only he had told me the truth. I thought maybe we could have been our own little secret. I never really understood sex till Flexing Star explained to me; he told me it had to be with someone you loved in order to understand. He said it wasn't always perfect, that it could be addicting and you should only do it when you are ready and under your own conditions.

In Fort McMurray, I tried to kill myself once and was almost sent away for it. I was not allowed to talk to Elaine or have access to a phone. After those restrictions, I started to feel trapped. I didn't have friends in Fort McMurray who remembered who I was because I hadn't lived there in a long time. I did have one friend who I'm going to call "Pothead." I talked to him and asked for a distraction. I snuck out with him and his friends. We walked to Dickins from Timbo because apparently that's where "the pot" was. We went there and baked our lungs. After, we decided to go to one of Pothead's friends' houses in Thickwood. Before we arrived, two of the guys we were with disappeared and we had to look for them. Apparently they had gone into an alley and the oldest guy amongst us had given the second oldest guy a blowjob for money to buy a hotdog.

One thing about some teenagers is that when we need money, and our parents are either too broke to give it to us or too stingy, we do things like flash people, give blowjobs and do body shots to get it. When we arrived at the friend's house we saw a guy lying on the ground. I thought he had passed out or else he was dead. We went and hit the dab pen; the pothead didn't know how strong it was and he gave it to me. I have a high tolerance so I didn't go crazy like he did. His friend ended up having to walk me home. He left me by the front gate; I had a cigarette and I wanted to smoke it because I knew I probably wouldn't get a chance like this again.

While I was outside smoking, two guys came and said they had pot and did I want some. I went over to their house and smoked some more. I got really high and things got loopy, and then they raped me. After they raped me, they ditched me by the gate where they found me. I got Natasha to open the door for me. My body was sore and I was shivering. I talked to Natasha and Brooklyn about it and they thought I should tell the authorities but then I felt I couldn't because I was doing drugs and not only legal drugs, illegal ones too. I started getting sick and throwing up. I had missed my period. Natasha asked her friend to go get me a pregnancy test and it came out positive. At school I took another test that another friend got for me and that came out positive, too. Brooklyn also got me a test but I didn't take that one because I got scared.

For a while, I denied that it happened but I kept having flashbacks that told me otherwise. I'd had sex before so I knew what it felt like after, and yes, I felt that feeling. Because of the positive tests I started to overthink things; I was mostly worried about what my family would do. I was not going to abort the child or give him or her up for adoption. I would take long showers to get the disgusting feeling off my body that was put into my mind. I felt sick. I was powerless the night it happened; I couldn't even protect myself. I lost the one thing I had control over. I became a toy. I then realized that maybe that's how Flexing Star felt about me, that maybe he only cared because he saw me as his toy. Everyone cares about their toys, from little babies to adults. They love their kiddie toys, sex toys and human toys. I felt worthless because I was under the influence and I was dressed like a "slut." I blamed myself for a while, then I started thinking that I overreacted. I felt like maybe what they did to me was fine, normal, and that "it was what it was." Besides, they were high, too, and we became friends, so I thought made I should just calm down and take it as a compliment.

But no matter how many times I told myself that it was fine, I wanted to kill myself, because I thought I was pregnant and that the baby belonged to one of my two rapists. One night I went into the kitchen and took a knife; Brooklyn saw it and stopped me. Two days later, we got to skip school to go to Edmonton for Brooklyn's cheer competition and my period came. I was *so* relieved that I wasn't pregnant. The adults wanted to stay in a hotel but stupid me suggested we stay at my parents' house. The thought that they might leave me with them had crossed my mind, but I really wanted to see Elaine. My cousin's family dropped me off and then they said they had to go because my cousin in Edmonton who was playing soccer got hurt and was in the hospital. I felt bad for him, but I also knew they were not going to come back for me. Apparently, they had always been going to dump me in the trash with my parents. I later found out that Brooklyn had told them about me trying to kill myself and it was too much for them to handle.

THE BEGINNING OF
A NEW START

They say it is always darkest before dawn and I now understand what that means. I started stealing money from people and using it for drugs. I pretended to be better and an angel but I was still the same sick-in-the-head child. My family then moved to St. Albert, the city of hockey bobbleheads. I was also forced to go to a Catholic school with conceited, racist, homophobic idiots. I got two birds; Chica and Flicker. Chica died in a fight with Flicker, and we got another bird named Tinker-Blue. I stopped taking antidepressants and stopped therapy.

In my opinion, therapists think they can fix you, they think that a broken glass can be fixed. But even if it can be fixed, it won't be the same; it will be viewed as the broken glass that needed help to be fixed. It is a weak label that I do not want to have. Other people who go to therapy will have their own views but this is mine. I read a book called *A Touching Spirit Bear*. It says that counsellors, psychologists, the government and parents are always trying to fix you but you can't fix or get rid of something that is part of you.

I also came to an interesting view about the BLM (Black Lives Matter) protests of 2020. I was in social studies class and we were talking about current events. I thought that it was crazy how no one couldn't care less for Black lives. In my lifetime I have been called racial slurs, my cousins and I have been threatened by a "Karen" for listening to rap music, and at school when I would tell teachers about racist comments other people made e, they would just say something like "You know how he is, he gets carried away; it's just his personality," as if being racist was a personality. No one cared until it became a trend, until a man lost his life. What about the lives that were lost way before George Floyd? Besides the Black Lives Matter irony, teachers are supposed to make sure their students feel safe. I had told my parents about all the bullying and they wanted to involve the police. I said they shouldn't. When you are a teenager, you can't be caught being a snitch—you will be tormented until you are driven to either leave the school or kill yourself. When I moved to St. Albert, I decided to join the Air Cadets so that I would be able to move out of my parents' house at the age of 16. My grandfather had served in the Zimbabwean military, I had an aunt in the military but my love of planes made me choose the Airforce route. Incidentally, when I joined the Air Cadets, I began to learn about leadership and honorable values.

The first days in St. Albert were terrible. I missed the school bus because I was talking to the counsellor, so I tried to walk home and I got lost. I had to walk five kilometres because the police still had my phone for the investigation. I ended up asking a stranger to call my mom to take me home. My dad also found my weed and wanted to call the police, but he couldn't because he knew he would be fined and everyone who knew I smoked would have gotten in trouble. I didn't have access to weed in St. Albert. There were kids who sold vapes but used ones—and people wonder why Covid cases keep increasing! When I couldn't find my weed, I cried because it was my escape, but I eventually got over it.

My parents eventually found out about the rape. Brooklyn had told the adults. She acts so humble and tricks you into opening up to her and then she ruins your life—or so I thought at the time. She would say, "I won't tell anyone, it's not my story to tell," and she is why I now have major trust issues. I'm not going to say that it's her fault completely, because it's my parents fault, too, as well as the fault of toxic boyfriends and toxic friends. Therapists say that talking helps; parents force you to talk and friends expect you to talk but like Clay Jensen says in the show *13 Reasons Why*, "If there was a fire in a house and you were in it, would you sit down and talk about it? Or would you get out of the fire?" Teenagers try to get out of the fire with or without anyone's help.

Some parents tell their kids that if they talk to other teenagers, it's burdening them, but to me that's BALONEY. Personally, I am always there for my fellow teenagers who are struggling. By telling a teenager that they shouldn't talk to their friends, you can make them feel like they don't have anyone in the world who understands them. No parent should be surprised if their depressed teenager kills themselves after they've told them that. It might be overwhelming for other kids to hear us talk about our problems, but teenagers who have a mental health disorder know when they are making someone uncomfortable or when they have overstepped. I have prevented people from suicide and their thoughts do not influence me. I have my own broken pieces, but they are separate and different from the people I helped out of suicide.

We get that parents were teenagers themselves once, but it's different now. During my parents' teenage years there was no social media. They didn't have to worry about what they looked like or what they said as much as we do. You could have a perfect teenager, with good looks, a defined body and good grades but they could still feel trapped. They could feel like they have to live up to the title given to them. I am not pretty and I don't have a defined body, but I did have good grades. I felt like I needed to have great grades in order to be valued. I felt like because I wasn't pretty or because I didn't have a sexy body, I was nothing; my grades defined who I was. People would call me "smartass" and my parents were proud, but I felt like I was trapped. I would do work in my free time and once I even did my friend's homework for her.

As for relationships, why are they such a big deal for teenagers? Well, a big part of it has to do with social media. Social media feeds us with false images of what a relationship should look like. I think the majority of teenagers know that what they're seeing could be false or only a cover, but we still aim to have relationships like those portrayed on social media. Teenagers try to have perfect and flawless relationships. I am not saying that social media corrupts teenage minds, but it does play a big part in making teenage-hood so hard. It feeds into making teenagers feel insecure, but it's nonetheless a huge part of being a teenager.

Technology and social media is a teenager's life; if a parent takes that away, they need to be prepared to face the beast they unleash. I had no technology or social media for a while and I went crazy—I became a delinquent. I felt that I might as well be in jail if my parents deprived me of my social media life. Teenagers have two lives: the real one and the social media one. On social media, they can look like a confident, humble, smart kid but in reality they are a broken, insecure antisocial kid. Social media gives a teenager the perfect life they want, an escape from reality. Teenagers love being in control. If someone takes their control away from them, they will react. Life is already hard for teenagers but trapping them and making them feel suffocated will not benefit you—you will be taking a hard L if you break a teenager. Besides breaking a teenager, you will be losing the tranquility in your household. If you do it purposefully to your teenager, be prepared to say *arrivederci* to his/her trust.

The experience for teenage boys could be a bit different than it is for teenage girls. Boys have this image set out for them by other boys. Boys are told to "man up" or that "boys don't cry." Part of the reason boys rape is because of the stereotypes and pressures put on them. Of course, it doesn't justify rape. Boys can control themselves—but they can't control the negative stereotypical comments they get from other boys.

In writing this book, I don't want to influence other teenagers to be like me, but I hope that other teenagers will learn from some of what

I learned and that parents will gain a better understanding of what we go through; that it's not easy for us teenagers. It all builds up from childhood experiences and the environment we grow up in. One thing I learned from my experiences is that I am a BADASS. I still haven't learned to control my emotions, but I have learned to control the way I react.

One day I woke up and I just said, "No. I can't live like this anymore. If I'm forced to go on living, I might as well live like the baddest bitch on earth." I realized that my anger comes from the people who hurt me, which fuels and motivates me to show those toxic people that I am NOT weak. I started watching YouTube videos about self-care. Adelaine Morin's videos inspire me. Her videos have shown me that I need to love myself. It's okay to feel the way I feel; I just need to pick myself up whenever I fall. I shouldn't depend on other people to be happy. I needed to become my best friend.

Now I look at myself in the mirror at the beginning of each day and the end of each day, hyping myself up. Even a quick walking-past-the-mirror "Ooh, damn I'm fine" like Cardi B says will make you feel good about yourself. When I feel sad and unmotivated, I cry first then take a nice cold shower and do some self-care things like shave, put on a facemask or do meditation or yoga. I never let myself go to bed crying or sad anymore; I will elevate my mood so that in the morning I won't feel sluggish.

Rosa Parks said, "Each person must live their life as a model for others." If I was the person I was in the past, then I'm no model but I've moved past that. The past is in the past and I have learned from it. It was hard to start feeling like a badass when my mood was always so low, but in one of Adelaine Morin's videos she says you just have to fake it till you make it, and that's why I did.

"The most alluring thing a woman can have is confidence," according to Beyoncé; Queen Bey, I am still working on my confidence. In order to feel like and be a badass, you need to have confidence and a positive mindset; you need to have a love-it-or-hate-it vibe like Nicki Minaj. Last but not least, you don't need a significant other to feel special; you are a beautiful, sexy badass and no one can tell you otherwise.

I'm sorry, I sincerely apologize. I am truly trying really hard to be better. I'm trying to have a positive outlook toward myself. I thought maybe if I loved myself, then others would love me, too, but that's not how it works, does it? People judge you for your past, not the path and journey you take to becoming emotionally, mentally and physically better. They don't see a fighter—they see someone dying in shame of the mess they made. Well, I'm done focusing on getting attention, being noticed. To others, I am invisible and they managed to make me believe that I'm invisible and I don't belong in this world. They made me think that I am the problem and that everything is my fault. Truth is, it's everyone's fault but my mine for dwelling on the mistakes and not moving past them. It is my fault for trying to get people to forgive me when I hadn't forgiven myself. I finally saw that I need to forgive myself for letting toxicity into my life, forgive myself for the nasty labels I gave myself, forgive myself for the horrible things I did to my body. I'm a fighter and it is my fight and I will win, whether anyone believes in me or not.

I'm sorry to myself for not knowing my worth and not knowing that I belong in this messed-up world with this messed-up society that will change because of me. I was put here to make a difference, to change society's ways, to patch up the holes and discard the flaws, and I will put an end to how individuals are treated based on their ethnicity, nationality, religion, or sexuality.

I am stepping off this roller coaster now.

www.ingramcontent.com/pod-product-compliance
Lightning Source LLC
LaVergne TN
LVHW011854060526
838200LV00054B/4331